Eleanor Berry is the author of nineteen books, but says her first brush with literature was when she broke windows in Ian Fleming's house at the age of eight. Of Welsh ancestry, she was born and bred in London, where she has lived all her life. She holds a BA Hons degree in English. After university Berry worked as a commercial translator, using French and Russian. She then worked as a research assistant to a Harley Street specialist and has since worked intermittently as a medical secretary. Two of her novels have been translated into Russian, and a third, which she refrains from naming, is currently being made into a film. This is her sixth book to be published by Book Guild Publishing.

She is the author of numerous articles in *The Oldie* magazine. Her interests, among others, include Russian literature, Russian folk songs, Irish rebel songs, the cinema, amateur piano playing and medicine.

Housebound Store

Reviews

Tell Us a Sick One Jakey
'This book is quite repulsive!' Sir Michael Havers, Attorney General

Never Alone with Rex Malone
'A ribald, ambitious black comedy, a story powerfully told.' Stewart Steven, *The Daily Mail*

'I was absolutely flabbergasted when I read it!' Robert Maxwell

The Ruin of Jessie Cavendish
'Eleanor Berry is to Literature what Hieronymus Bosch is to Art. As with all Miss Berry's books, the reader has a burning urge to turn the page.' Sonia Drew, *The International Continental Review*

Your Father Died on the Gallows
'A unique display of black humour which somehow fails to depress the reader.' Craig McLittle, *The Rugby Gazette*

Cap'n Bob and Me
'One of the most amusing books I have read for a long time. Eleanor Berry is an original.' Elisa Segrave, *The Literary Review*

'Undoubtedly the most amusing book I have read all year.' Julia Llewellyn-Smith, *The Times*

'A comic masterpiece.' *The Times*

Alandra Varinia, Seed of Sarah
'Eleanor Berry manages to maintain her raw and haunting wit as much as ever.' Dwight C. Farr, *The Texas Chronicle*

Jaxton the Silver Boy
'This time Eleanor Berry tries her versatile hand at politics. Her sparkling wit and the reader's desire to turn the page are still in evidence. Eleanor Berry is unique.' Don F. Saunderson, *The South London Review*

Someone's Been Done Up Harley
'In this book, Eleanor Berry's dazzling wit hits the Harley Street scene. Her extraordinary humour had me in stitches.' Thelma Masters, *The Oxford Voice*

O Hitman, My Hitman!
'Eleanor Berry's volatile pen is at it again. This time, she takes her readers back to the humorously eccentric Harley Street community. She also introduces Romany gypsies and travelling circuses, a trait which she has inherited from her self-confessed gypsy aunt, the late writer, Eleanor Smith, after whom she is named. Like Smith, Berry is an inimitable and delightfully natural writer.' Kev Zein, *The Johannesburg Evening Sketch*

McArandy was Hanged on the Gibbet High
'We have here a potboiling, swashbuckling blockbuster, which is rich in adventure, intrigue, history, amorous episodes and black humour. The story Eleanor Berry tells is multi-coloured, multi-faceted and nothing short of fantastic.' Angel Z. Hogan, *The Daily Melbourne Times*

The Scourging of Poor Little Maggie
'This harrowing, tragic and deeply ennobling book caused me to weep for two days after reading it.' Moira McClusky, *The Cork Evening News*

The Revenge of Miss Rhoda Buckleshott
'Words are Eleanor Berry's toys and her use of them is boundless.' Mary Hickman, professional historian and writer

The Most Singular Adventures of Eddy Vernon
'Rather a hot book for bedtime.' Nigel Dempster, *The Daily Mail*

The Maniac in Room 14
'This is the funniest book I've read for months.' Samantha Morris, *The Exeter Daily News*

Stop the Car, Mr Becket!
'This book makes for fascinating reading, as strange and entertaining as Eleanor Berry's other books which came out before it.' Gaynor Evans, *The Bristol Evening Post*

Take it Away, It's Red
'Despite the sometimes weighty portent of this book, a sense of subtle, dry and powerfully engaging humour reigns throughout its pages. The unexpected twist is stupendous.' Stephen Carson, *The Carolina Sun*

The House of Weird Doctors
'This delightful medical caper puts even A.J. Cronin in the shade.' Noel I. Leskin, *The Stethoscope*

Sixty Funny Stories
'This book is a laugh a line. Eleanor Berry is truly unique.'
Elisa Segrave, famous diarist and writer.

THE MOST SINGULAR ADVENTURES OF SARAH LLOYD

'A riotous read from start to finish.'
Ned McMurphy, *The Irish Times*

Eleanor Berry
www.eleanorberry.net

Book Guild Publishing
Sussex, England

First published in Great Britain in 2008 by
The Book Guild Ltd
Pavilion View
19 New Road
Brighton, East Sussex
BN1 1UF

Typesetting in Baskerville by
Keyboard Services, Luton, Bedfordshire

Printed in Great Britain by
Athenaeum Press Ltd, Gateshead

A catalogue record for this book is available from
The British Library

ISBN 978 1 84624 266 3

Contents

For my cousin, Juliet (Varinia, goddess of wit)

Part I

The Biddle Family

It was January 1995. The weather was stormy and windy and the sky was battleship grey.

The house the Biddle family intended to settle down in, after fifteen years in a polluted Liverpool, was twenty miles south of Dublin. The Biddles travelled in a navy blue Volvo with a banal notice which read, 'My other car is a Rolls-Royce' in the back window.

Edward Biddle, the head of the Biddle family, was a solicitor like his father and grandfather. He had a vast inheritance to supplement his salary. He was neither handsome nor ugly. He had a somewhat craggy face with wavy brown hair and brown eyes. The Biddles had lived in a pleasant, four storey-house overlooking the Mersey.

The family's pleasure was short-lived. A heinous, red-brick crematorium, permanently belching its sooty dead, spoiling the sky, blocked the Biddles's sensational view that had given them so much happiness. The value of the property slumped. Biddle decided to leave Liverpool and take up farming in Southern Ireland, from which his distant relations on his mother's side had hailed.

Biddle had married Alice while both were training to be solicitors. He was attracted by her shyness, frailty and long silences but failed to recognise her stupidity and overall boringness until well into the marriage. Biddle

1

had married Alice because he liked to dominate conversations without being interrupted.

The Biddles had two identical twin daughters, aged seventeen. Their father had arranged for them to train at a secretarial college in Dublin. Their names were Hannah and Mary and though identical in looks, they had different personalities and intellects. Hannah was clever, ambitious and precocious, and hoped eventually to enter Trinity College, Dublin, to read Philosophy. Mary, on the other hand, had no interests at all, not even in child-bearing and housework. Both had wavy, brown, layered hair and brown eyes but neither had particularly pretty faces, although when Hannah used make-up, she was prettier than her sister. The twins seldom quarrelled and because they had nothing in common, they avoided each other's company as much as they could.

Alice had not spoken since they arrived across the water. She sat in the passenger's seat, thinking nothing. Mary, similar in character to her mother, sat in the back, vacantly staring into space. A golden Labrador, called Toby, lay asleep between the twins. Hannah hugged and caressed him throughout the journey, while talking animatedly to her father. Mary ignored the dog and stared at the floor.

Mulligan Manor, a rambling, desolate house, had been painted white years ago and stood alone, unaccompanied by any other houses, menacingly overlooking a bleak, forlorn valley. Its name had been chosen by its only long-term owner, Seamus O'Rafferty, because its initials matched Marilyn Monroe's and O'Rafferty had always had an eye for tragic women.

The house was approached by a sinuous, overgrown drive and as it grew closer, Hannah suddenly leant forward with her head between her knees, feeling sick. Mary reacted in a different way. Instead of sharing the ghostly

2

premonition which preoccupied Hannah, she felt no sense of the sinister or the evil.

Apart from the weird feeling she experienced, Hannah was excited by the new life that lay ahead of her, learning to type and take shorthand, going to Trinity College and settling down as a journalist or a writer, preferably with a husband.

The power of the Volvo suddenly cut out a hundred yards away from the house. Biddle swore softly, got out of the car and raised the bonnet.

'Mary, get the torch from the boot, will you?'

Mary got out and opened the boot. She couldn't see the torch although it was in the corner and because of its size, it stared her straight in the face.

'Sorry, I can't find it.'

Biddle was unable to shake off the bronchitis he had had for three weeks and had a fit of coughing which made the pain in his chest worse and his temper worse still. He strode round to the boot and found the torch straight away. He gave his daughter a clip on the ear.

'God, you're stupid, Mary!'

Mary showed no reaction. She got back into the car with her head bowed and gently shut the door.

Hannah felt a sudden sense of shame at having such a boring, stupid sister.

'Hey, you with the brain! You haven't shut the door.'

Mary opened the door and slammed it violently. Biddle, still in a violent temper, wrenched it open.

'How dare you slam one of my doors like that!' He grabbed her by the arm and dragged her out of the car. 'Make the rest of your way on foot!' he shouted.

Mary obeyed her father without speaking. She hadn't told anyone, not even anyone in her family, what had happened to her a year ago. The shock magnified within her as the days passed by. She felt that she had had enough of life and wouldn't have cared if she'd died then.

Mary knew she was stupid and unable to make her plain face pretty in the way her sister could. She only had one O level. She had never read a book in her life as the written word daunted her. She had never seen a play, attended a concert or visited an art gallery. She could not play a musical instrument, compose a story in her native tongue or even account for the money she spent. This was something her father asked her to do every week, to justify an increase in her allowance. Because of her incompetence, her allowance remained low and the only clothes she bought were damp-smelling hand-me-downs from Oxfam shops.

Unlike her precocious twin sister, who took contraceptives and who had bedded a large number of boys at her school, Mary had no confidence in herself. The opposite sex seldom sought her company, and because she slouched about with as much hair covering her face as possible to hide her plainness, and uttered so few words, few people showed an interest in her, other than her family, who nagged her constantly about how to make herself look more attractive.

Mary hardly ever cried. She had not even cried since her trauma a year ago. She walked towards the house and sat cross-legged outside the front door, supporting her chin with her hand, ignoring the cold weather.

Biddle started the Volvo. He was baffled by the fact that there was nothing wrong with it. He was equally surprised to see Mary sitting outside the front door, without an overcoat in a temperature of almost zero. A surge of guilt and sorrow went through him. This was the first time in his life that he concluded that his daughter was mentally disturbed, without anyone telling him what had happened to her. A tender and loving pity raced through him.

'Come on, Mary. Daddy didn't mean to speak to you

like that. You'll feel much better when we get inside. It's a lovely house, isn't it?'

Mary appeared not to have heard. Her eyes were out of focus and stared inwards at each other. Biddle was alarmed and afraid to ask her what was wrong with her. He thought that her ailment might be a women's matter.

'I know there's something wrong. You can tell me.'

'It happened last year. It's too bad to tell anyone.'

'I've told the housekeeper, Mrs Gallagher, to make up fires in all the grates. We'll have tea with toast and treacle before getting everything ready. Come on, try and give us all a hand unloading the car.'

Biddle's kind words had an unexpected effect on his sick daughter. She felt tears coming into her eyes.

'You can't go on sitting there. You'll get piles.'

He took her hand to pull her up and Mary, identically dressed to her twin sister in grey, denim dungarees, covering a thick, mauve, polo-neck sweater, allowed her father to pull her up, aware that he loved her but no longer caring.

'Come on, Mary,' called Hannah. 'You can't leave all the work to us.'

Biddle went over to Hannah who was reaching up to remove things from the roof-rack.

'I won't tolerate your being unkind to Mary any more, Hannah. She's very sick and she needs a family's love.'

'Sick? In what way?'

'Mary's mentally ill. Something ghastly happened to her not too long ago. I don't think she's genuinely stupid and it must be bitterly hurtful to be called stupid.'

'It was you who called her "stupid", Daddy, not me.'

'That's as may be. The main thing is that we must all be very kind to her. Once we're sorted out, we'll find a psychiatrist in Dublin. In the meantime, you be nice to her. Do you understand?'

5

Hannah pinched her cheeks to which she had just applied some rouge and touched her eyelashes to make sure that her mascara was dry.

'Of course I understand. I had no idea.'

'And for God's sake, try to get out of her what happened to her. I suspect that that will be a woman's job.'

'OK, Daddy.'

Mary went over to Hannah and helped her to unload the roof-rack.

'Well done, Mary, you're doing a great job. By the way, sorry I wasn't very nice earlier. I didn't mean it. Besides, there's no need to hide anything from me. I've heard that something very unpleasant happened to you not so long ago. I'm your twin sister and you must rely on me to put right what's wrong. Whatever happens you must tell me the truth.'

With the help of Mrs Gallagher and her strapping, farm-hand sons, the Biddles moved into the house.

'Hannah, will you go out and check that there's nothing in the car?' said Biddle. 'I know we're missing something.'

Hannah found Toby, the golden Labrador, lying on the floor in the back, howling with terror. She was afraid that he was injured and looked at his paws, ears, stomach and legs but found no cause for his pain. She pulled him by the collar to get him out but he refused to move and his howling became even louder.

'Mary, can you come over and help me, please? Toby won't get out. Can you bring something to tie him with?' called Hannah.

'What the hell's all this rubbish?' asked Biddle. 'We all want to go to bed. Get Toby out and bring him indoors.'

'We can't. He won't move,' said Hannah.

Biddle reached into the car and picked Toby up, not realizing how heavy he was. Toby gave a strange, long scream which left Biddle stone cold. He carried the dog

6

down a dark, linoleum-floored corridor, leading to the hall.

The situation got worse. Toby came out in a cold sweat, so concentrated that it soaked Biddle's clothes. He assumed that the dog had suddenly contracted a virus and because he was poorly informed about canine illnesses, he suspected that it was fatal and panicked. He screamed for Hannah, the only practical member of the family.

'For Christ's sake help me! Toby's dying.'

'Dying? He was all right in the car.'

'This has just come on. What do I do?'

Hannah caressed Toby who quivered in her father's arms. The temperature in the small, dark corridor suddenly dropped ten degrees. The flabbergasted father and daughter thought that this was no more than a bad dream.

A jet of blood spurted from the dog's mouth. The father and daughter stood frozen against the wall. Yet more blood began to flow and Toby's former robust shrieks were reduced to the type of frail moaning that precedes death.

Biddle rushed to the lodge at the bottom of the drive, carrying Toby, accompanied by Hannah. She banged repeatedly on the door of the lodge, encouraged to see the light on. Finnegan, the lodge keeper and minder of the estate, was in his sixties and not very bright. He looked older than his sixty odd years and had worked on the estate in O'Rafferty's day.

'First, I'll introduce myself and my daughter,' said Biddle, so out of breath he could hardly speak. A severe wheezing sound came from his chest as if he had pneumonia. 'I'm Edward Biddle, the new owner of Mulligan Manor and this is my daughter, Hannah.'

Finnegan removed his cap and greeted them, looking very puzzled, without asking why the dog was bleeding from the mouth.

7

Biddle slapped both his hands on Finnegan's shoulders. 'Our dog's bleeding to death. For God's sake find us a vet in Dublin,' he gasped.

Finnegan looked frightened and screwed up his tiny, blue eyes. 'There's only one place that runs an all-night, veterinary service in Dublin. Get the car and I'll show you the way.'

'I'm afraid to take the car. It keeps breaking down,' said Biddle.

'I have a tractor. We'll be going straight away. I'll take you both but you'll have to sit on the mudguards.'

'I'm very grateful to you, Mr Finnegan,' said Biddle.

The journey to Dublin was no enviable experience. Biddle sat on one mudguard clinging to Toby, and Hannah sat on the other side, shouting words of encouragement to her father. The tractor lurched violently as it hit a pothole on the poorly-maintained road. Toby and Biddle fell off and he uttered some foul language in the hearing of Finnegan who instinctively crossed himself.

The all-night vet lived and worked in the red-light district of Dublin. Biddle was so exhausted and miserable that he was afraid to hold Toby too close, fearing he was dead. He tumbled from the tractor a second time, not bothering to wait for Finnegan to help him down.

Hannah eased herself down and rushed over to Toby.

'He's better, Daddy. The bleeding's stopped and his breathing's OK.'

Biddle's behind ached from sitting on the mudguard. The pain was so extreme that for a moment he no longer cared whether Toby was dead or alive. Just then, he longed to be at home, enjoying his conjugal rights which were all that his half-witted wife could offer him.

A mini-skirted prostitute sidled up to him as he sat on the pavement, rocking from side to side to ease his pain.

'Would you be wanting a good time, sir?'

'Not a lot,' snarled Biddle. 'I don't want to get VD.'

His English accent stood out among the gathering of inquisitive Dubliners. The prostitute put her hands on her hips and threw back her mane of black hair, flashing her small-pupilled, beady, blue eyes.

'Bloody Brit!'

Biddle's temper worsened and he went straight for Finnegan.

'Come on, Mr Finnegan, which way now? We haven't got all night!'

Finnegan rang one of the bells in a tattered-looking, high-rise block.

'Cassidy speaking.'

'Mr Cassidy. This is Finnegan from Mulligan Manor. We've got a sick dog here, so sick he might die!'

'Do come in, Mr Finnegan.'

He and the Biddles rode to the eighteenth floor in a foul-smelling lift, daubed with anti-British graffiti, some of it mild, some of it vitriolic. Cassidy was a smiling, white-haired man in a dazzling, white coat, his face pink and clean-shaven. The rest of his person was soap-scented and well-groomed which contrasted refreshingly with the filthy lift. He introduced himself to the Biddles, caressed the dog and raised it gently on to an enamel-topped table. Cassidy stared for a while at Toby, probing his coat, paws and ears.

'So what seems to be the trouble with this fine, glossy gentleman?' he asked.

Biddle gave an emotional explanation and he, Hannah and Finnegan were offered tea by Cassidy's female assistant. Cassidy looked down the dog's throat with a torch, and investigated with cold, sterilized instruments. He could find nothing wrong and looked baffled. He checked Toby's breathing in case of obstruction and found nothing abnormal. The dog started to lick his hands and wag his tail.

'There doesn't seem to be much wrong with your dog, Mr Biddle, but I'll have to do a test to find out why the bleeding started. I'll be giving him an emetic in case he's swallowed something he shouldn't have.'

Biddle was exhausted and no longer cared about the dog's illness. 'That's fine, Mr Cassidy,' he muttered.

The dog was sick within ten minutes and brought up a lot of blood. Cassidy looked puzzled. He dried a sample of blood on a slide and put it under a microscope, where he saw millions of particles of ground glass. Cassidy had some idea what was wrong. He went next door and ushered Biddle and Hannah in.

'What's wrong with my dog?' asked Biddle.

Cassidy removed his spectacles and held them in the air. 'Mr Biddle, am I right in thinking you have just moved into Mulligan Manor?'

'Yes. Why do you ask?'

'I happened to be practising in Mr O'Rafferty's day. I often looked after his animals when they were sick.'

'I'm sure that's very interesting.'

'I know you are exhausted, Mr Biddle and I can well understand why you might be a little irritable. What I am trying to say is this: get out of that place while you can. It's not a happy house. It does not like people.'

'Don't give me a load of crap, Mr Cassidy. I've been travelling since four this morning. What the hell are you talking about? I'm not superstitious.'

'Just before you start laying into me, I feel I must ask you a question: did you take your dog down a dark, linoleum-floored corridor?'

'Well, as a matter of fact I did. What's all this in aid of?'

'No one has dared to live at Mulligan Manor since Seamus O'Rafferty's day. No one will stand it. There was worse blood in his family than in any family I've ever known. My advice to you is seal the corridor off and auction the house.'

Biddle's irritability increased while Hannah tried to calm him down.

'What's that got to do with my dog bringing up blood and glass?'

Cassidy mopped the sweat from his brow. Biddle's impatient behaviour made him nervous. He was more accustomed to having his fellow countrymen as clients, rather than Englishmen who were so often rude, demanding and peremptory.

'Mr Biddle, your manner is making me very alarmed. I can tell you a little but I can't tell you all because a curse would be put on me if I did. I advise you to seal that corridor off straight away. I have nothing further to tell you about your dog.'

'This man, Seamus O'Rafferty – what sort of a man was he?' asked Biddle, deliberately making his voice more gentle.

Cassidy smiled as if describing a woman. 'He was a man of extraordinary physical beauty, so much so that women often fainted when meeting him for the first time.'

Hannah suddenly perked up. Cassidy continued. 'He was also known to be a bully with a violent temper but underneath, he had a heart of gold. Love is blind, Mr Biddle,' said Cassidy, his eyes suddenly wet with tears. 'Love is blind. Mr O'Rafferty had no control over what was happening in his house. He often beat his children in his study. He beat them because they tried to tell him what was wrong to make it stop.'

'What *was* wrong?' asked Biddle, now intrigued rather than irritated.

'You must forgive me, Mr Biddle. A last Will and Testament was made, of which a small amount was passed on to me. I was sworn to silence. If you take an oath, you rot in hell if you don't keep to it.'

'You must understand, Mr Cassidy,' said Biddle, forcing himself to be patient, 'I've taken a lot of trouble getting my family here. I have no intention of moving out and if my dog doesn't care for my domestic arrangements, I'll have a kennel built for him outside. I'm not sealing my corridor off but if it will satisfy you, I'll tell my family not to use it.'

Cassidy turned his back on Biddle and wiped the enamel table with a cloth. He found Biddle patronizing and disrespectful to his trade.

'If that is the case, Mr Biddle, I fear that we will meet again in circumstances less happy than these.'

The Biddles started walking towards the door with the dog. Cassidy handed a scruffy piece of paper to Biddle. 'This is my bill for seventy-five guineas, sir.'

'What, for coming to a horrible building like this?

Cassidy sidled towards Biddle, rubbing his fingers together, his voice scarcely above a whisper. 'You'll have to pardon me, Mr Biddle, but we Irish have to charge Brits more than ourselves. You've shackled us for hundreds of years. We see to it that you pay for that, whoever you are.'

Biddle was exhausted, but instead of losing his temper he tried humour instead of aggression. 'Come now, my dear chap, you can't blame me for that. The trouble was started by King Henry II of England in 1172, no doubt to take his mind off Becket's murder two years earlier.'

It was only when Biddle was about to fall asleep that he embarked on rambling, unsolicited information.

The bludgeoned vet smiled.

'I admire your knowledge of history, sir. Besides, the words that I uttered were only in jest. My fee is the same for all my clients, no matter what race.'

Biddle smiled. Cassidy gave him his card.

'Be sure to ring me tomorrow and let me know how

your dog is. But take my advice. What I told you about your house is no old wives' tale.'

A half-finished chocolate cake lay on a plate on a side table. The evacuation of his stomach had made Toby hungry. He got on to his hind legs and wolfed it down, wagging his tail. Biddle struggled to keep a straight face but apologized to Cassidy with whom he shook hands amicably, thinking that he was a nut. Finnegan went home on the tractor, leaving the Biddles to take a taxi.

Alice and Mary had already eaten a tinned meal, washed down by claret, served by Rita, a slow-moving, drugged-looking cook who lived off the premises. They had gone to bed by the time the other two arrived. The sisters had been assigned a small, double room, overlooking the bleak, rocky valley. Mary had insomnia and was awake when her sister arrived. Hannah rarely tired easily and felt the need to talk to her sister.

Mary raised herself, supporting herself by her elbows. 'Is there any more news about Toby? Is he going to be all right?' she asked.

'He already is all right. You should have seen what he did at the vet's. He leapt onto a table and ate some chocolate cake. The vet found nothing wrong with him but he did tell us something awfully strange. He said he used to look after Seamus O'Rafferty's animals and that we are the first people to live in this house since his death. That's a good twenty years ago. Apparently, there's something not quite right about this house. There was something evil here and a lot of bad blood. That's why no one's dared live here.'

'What's all this about?' asked Mary, trying to take her mind off her trauma.

'I'll tell you more tomorrow. Since we're both wide awake, I want to talk to you about something else. First, I want you to drink the whisky I've brought up for you. Put the pillows under your head and lie down.'

Mary lay down and Hannah raised the glass full of whisky and water to her sister's lips. Within five minutes, she felt more comfortable. Hannah held her hand.

'You must tell me, Mary. What happened to you to make you so disturbed? You've got to tell me, however bad it was, and you'll feel so much better once it's off your chest.'

* * *

Hannah and Mary looked so alike that they were put in different classes in their co-educational school in Liverpool. Hannah had slept with nearly all the boys in her class and rather than being envious of her, the girls regarded her as being a 'bit of a lass'.

Mary's classroom was next door to Hannah's and had an equal number of students. They were studying Shakespeare's *Julius Caesar* of which Mary couldn't understand a word. She had a crush on a boy called Colin Jackson who had an olive-green complexion, beady, bright green eyes and jet black, greased-back hair like Elvis Presley's. She wondered whether he was going out with anyone but was too shy to ask. Instead, she would stare at his profile across the room, her heart hammering against her ribs. One day, he caught her eye and smiled. She blushed and lowered her mouse-like head into *Julius Caesar*.

Miss Clarke, taking the class, noticed her inattentiveness. 'Mary Biddle, could you please tell us who Brutus's best friend was?'

Mary couldn't answer. Shakespeare had always confused her. Jackson was winking at her.

'Cassius,' he mouthed.

'Well, Mary?' asked Miss Clarke.

'Cassius, miss.'

A note, screwed up in a ball landed on her desk. 'I

fancy you, Mary, because you're not like other people. Let's meet for a drink tonight – Col.'

Mary turned the colour of a lobster. She returned the note with her affirmative reply. She waited until the end of school, her heart rattling out loud and her hands trembling. Jackson was waiting for her outside. She regarded her virginity as a venereal disease and prayed that Jackson would deflower her that evening.

They went to a rowdy pub with pop music blaring and the air filled with wafting currents of smoke. Mary asked for a double whisky, followed by another and another to shed her inhibitions. Jackson, wearing a leather waistcoat and frayed, tight jeans, asked her to dance and held her firmly to let her feel his virility.

'Let's get out of here, Mare.'

She let him take her by the arm and stared at him lecherously. She knew that she had fallen in love with him.

'How about it, Mare? Fancy a poke with the dick?'

Mary gave a short, nervous laugh and her voice went an octave higher. 'I would,' she muttered awkwardly.

He took her to a disused warehouse, kissing her shoulder all the way. She was emboldened by the whisky and her personality was totally transformed. She leapt up onto him and kissed him passionately, putting her tongue in his mouth and licking his teeth. She discovered by the lumps of food between them and the foul smell of his breath that he had not cleaned his teeth for several days. Further, she had no idea that, at that time, girls were not supposed to play white and had to wait for the male to make the first move.

'Hey, not so fast, Mare. Come on, let's lie down.'

Still feverishly roused, she knelt at his feet and undid his zip. This time, he surrendered and lowered her to the stony floor, removed what clothing of hers that was

15

necessary to perform the sex act comfortably and entered her.

The pain was more than she could endure and she couldn't contain her tears. He swore under his breath and withdrew.

'Why didn't you tell me you'd never done this before?' snapped Jackson.

'I was ashamed to.'

He leant against the wall with one leg bent and lit a cigarette. 'I hate this place. I'm going home. Thanks for giving me such a good time,' he said unpleasantly.

Mary ran home, weeping out loud, feeling like a leper. The thing she dreaded most was Hannah finding out that she was a virgin and teasing her about it.

The worst was still to come. As she entered the classroom the next day, the students laughed and pointed at her. They banged their copies of *Julius Caesar* on their desks and started chanting: 'Virgin Mary! Virgin Mary!'

Mary ran outside. For some perverse reason, she retraced her steps to the warehouse where Jackson had taken her, with intent to cry the whole incident out of her system.

Three out-of-work thugs in their late teens happened to be in the warehouse at that time. They were drinking rum and passing the bottle to each other. They had on shabby, leather-studded jackets and one of them wore mirror-lens glasses so Mary couldn't tell whether he was looking at her or not. Terrified, she ran to the doorway but her exit was blocked by the thug in the mirror-lens glasses.

'Please! I'm not well. Please let me go home.'

'Not well, eh? What's it this time, VD?' said the thug.

'For God's sake, what harm have I ever done you?'

'We're mates of Colin Jackson. He says that you let him down last night,' said another of the thugs.

16

'How do you know him?' asked Mary.

'We drink in the same place. You're the famous Virgin Mary, aren't you? Why didn't you ask Colin to buy you a halo? Don't worry about your virginity. We'll soon loosen you up. That way, you won't be able to let people down in future.'

Mary blacked out after that. When she came round, she found that she was bleeding heavily between the legs and felt unbearably sore. Her mind was gone. Even in her head, she couldn't find any words. She lay on the stone floor for two hours and only came out of the warehouse because she was hungry.

* * *

Hannah was in tears by the end of Mary's story and continued to hold her hand.

'You're going to be all right now, Mare. If it's any consolation to you, I screwed that Jackson fellow myself and he took over three quarters of an hour to ejaculate. He also had gruesome halitosis so you didn't miss a thing.'

Mary sat up and wept on Hannah's shoulder and Hannah rocked her backwards and forwards.

'You're going to get over this. Not only that, Daddy's going to find a good psychiatrist in Dublin and I'm sure he'll put you right.'

It was two a.m. by the time the sisters had finished talking but Hannah was still feeling wide awake. She kept her bedside light on and lay on her stomach to read a gripping part which she had reached in a novel by James Hadley Chase.

Mary was exhausted but couldn't sleep with the light on. She wandered round the house until she found an unoccupied bedroom to be used as her parents' dressing room, next to their bedroom. She rolled into bed and fell into a dreamless sleep.

17

At four a.m. she woke up abruptly. The temperature of the room suddenly became colder. It dropped another ten degrees and she no longer felt comfortable. She picked up the mat near the bed and was about to put it on top of her blankets. The excessively cold temperature rose dramatically within a few seconds, as if being controlled by an invisible force concerned with her welfare. A strange peace took over her spirit and the gloom, which had been static since she had been raped, was no longer there. The peace enabled her to fall into a deep sleep. She had a strange dream in which she heard a rasping, male voice with a harsh but not unattractive Dublin accent. It was almost an Irish tinker's accent.

'Welcome to this house, Mary my friend. You've been very ill but you're going to recover.'

In the dream, Mary was startled but not afraid. Her slow reactions prevented her from having the initiative to answer. The outline of a form appeared before her as she slept. As it grew clearer, she saw a broad-shouldered man in his fifties, with large, liquid, grey eyes, unusually long lashes for a male, thick, dark hair and a loosened tie with the top two buttons of his shirt undone. Mary found this latter feature very appealing.

'Please, sir, tell me who you are,' she said out loud in her sleep.

'I was the last owner of this house. You will find out more as you continue to live here. You've suffered more than a decent young lady deserves.'

Mary found the man devastatingly attractive with his thick, Irish accent and gentlemanly manner. He excited her far more than Colin Jackson had. She woke up suddenly and sat up, longing to continue the dream, but when she slept again the man had disappeared.

She told herself that she would not mention her dream to anyone, not even Hannah. The twins came down to

18

breakfast at nine a.m. Hannah had prominent, black circles under her eyes from reading all night but Mary was uncharacteristically freshened and relaxed. Biddle had risen at dawn to see the farm manager, taking Toby with him, but Alice remained in bed, where she intended to stay all day.

The twins wolfed down their eggs, bacon and coffee.

'I know I'm going to like this house,' Mary said suddenly.

'You're crazy!' retorted her sister. 'Can't you tell it's haunted?'

'I don't think it is.' Mary was still determined not to speak of her dream. 'Let's go for a walk later on.'

'I'd like that – anything to get out of here. I'm going up to see if Mummy's all right first, Mare.'

Mary didn't answer. She finished her coffee and went to the living room where she stood by the window, overlooking the valley. She had a fantasy about the man in her dream riding across the valley on a savage, black horse, delivering her from the thugs who had raped her. She imagined him picking her up and letting her ride in front with him.

Hannah knocked on the door of her parents' bedroom, feeling an atmosphere of coldness and evil.

'Mummy, is there anything wrong?' she asked.

Alice was lying on her back, looking at the ceiling. There was a look of terror in her eyes and she shook all over as if she had a fever.

'What's the matter?' asked Hannah.

Alice's breathing grew faster. She wiped her sweating forehead with the sheet.

'There's something ghastly about this house,' she said. 'I can feel it in every room. All through the night, I've heard doors slamming, and people shouting and weeping. The whole place is alive with misery. I wish we'd never come.'

'Oh, come on, Mummy. You had a bad dream. People often have bad dreams when they sleep in a new place for the first time. Why don't you get up? It's a lovely day. We can go for a walk in the garden.'

'I'm not getting up. I'm staying here all day. I hate Ireland. I want to go home.'

'Don't you think you're being a bit silly? We've only just moved in. Won't you at least give it a try?' said Hannah patiently.

Alice rolled her head from side to side which irritated Hannah who considered this to be a display of amateur dramatics.

'There's something else I haven't told you, Hannah,' said Alice. 'I've been a teetotaller all my life. In fact, I've never tasted an alcoholic drink, but for some reason I have a yearning, even at this time of the morning, to drink alcohol.'

Because of the unexplained terror that Hannah had experienced just before going into her parents' room, she too knew that there was something sinister about the house but was determined not to tell her neurotic, unintelligent mother.

'I'll leave you to rest a little more. I'll pull down the blinds. You'll feel better after you've had some rest.'

Alice started screaming.

'No! No! Don't leave me in the dark!'

'All right. I'll leave you in daylight and you can have the bedside light on as well.'

'Hannah, dear?'

'Yes.'

'Please get a doctor. I'm so frightened.'

'Did Daddy say anything about all this?'

'No. He slept all night. He got up at dawn and went to see the farm manager.'

'OK. I'll get a doctor.'

Hannah moved towards the door.

20

'Don't leave me!' shouted the mother.

The girl suddenly became irritable. 'How the hell can I get a doctor without leaving the room? There's no telephone in here. I'll send Mary up to sit with you if you're scared.'

Mary was still looking out of the window in the living room, having fantasies about the man in her dream. She was about to wander round the house to find further signs of him. Her pleasant thoughts were interrupted by her sister who rushed into the room.

'Help me, Mary. God knows what's going on here but Mummy's ill in some way. She's got it into her head that the house is evil and she wants a doctor.'

'I've got an idea,' said Mary. 'I've found out that the doctor who looked after Seamus and Melissa O'Rafferty still practises in Dublin. He's getting on a bit but he still makes home visits.'

'Who told you that?'

'The cook last night, when you were taking Toby to Dublin.'

Hannah had no interest in psychic phenomena and although she knew that the house was haunted, she was getting thoroughly bored with the whole situation.

'Where's the phone?'

Mary beckoned her sister into a dusty room, once used as a study. Half-empty bottles, covered with cobwebs and dust, stood on an unused drinks' tray. A fireplace with a leather-studded fender supported by brass legs surrounded a pile of cold ashes and dust. An unframed, old photograph of an astonishingly beautiful girl in her late teens, with a lustrous mane of long, black hair cut in layers and liquid, grey eyes, stood on the mantelpiece.

This was Eileen O'Rafferty, who could bring a smile to her father's face when he was in a rage. Next to it, was an equally old photograph of an eight-year-old boy with a sweet face, lit up by a mischievous smile and pink cheeks. Paddy O'Rafferty was Eileen's kid brother and favourite sibling and O'Rafferty's favourite son.

When Hannah saw this photograph, she shuddered and her blood turned cold. She wondered whether this innocent-looking child might be the root of the evil that seemed to her to flow through the house like a polluted river.

Mary was still unconscious of any evil in the house.

'He's a sweet boy, isn't he, Hannah?' she remarked.

An old fashioned switchboard, similar to the models used in offices in the 1950s, stood by the window. It too, was covered with dust. Mary wiped it clean with her handkerchief.

'Can you work this thing, Hannah?'

'No. God, I hate the atmosphere in this room! It feels like that dark corridor we were advised to seal off. It's that boy. Whatever it is in here, seems to be coming from him.'

'Sounds like a load of rot to me,' said Mary.

'Can't you feel the horrible atmosphere in this room?'

'Not in the least. I think there's a pleasant atmosphere in here, apart from the dust which is making me cough.'

Hannah was astounded that Mary, who was normally so timid and mentally frail, should fail to notice the evil atmosphere.

'You get the switchboard to work, Mary. I'm getting out of here. This room gives me the creeps.'

Once Hannah had left the room, Mary's feeling of peace and pleasure increased to the point of being erotic. She had never seen a switchboard before. She stared vacantly at it for some time and found a dirty, white label on which the word 'cook' could be seen in neat, forward-slanting letters. She pressed down the switch.

'Rita speaking,' replied an unfriendly voice.

'I'm sorry to disturb you. It's Mary Biddle. It was such a nice dinner you cooked last night. I need the name and phone number of the doctor in Dublin who used to look after the O'Rafferty's.'

Although the cook had been complimented on her dinner, she remained surly and abrupt. This was because she was in the middle of preparing lunch and had no idea when Biddle would be back from the farm, or if Mrs Biddle would be well enough to come down.

'Dr Ryan, Dublin 251 1284,' rasped the cook.

'I know you must be busy but can you tell me how to dial out? I've never used one of these machines before.'

'Oh, for Jaysus's sake, Miss Biddle, can you not tell I'm busy? Press down the switch furthest to the left.'

Mary rang the surgery and told the secretary that her mother had some mysterious illness.

'Where do you live, Miss Biddle?'

'At Mulligan Manor, where Seamus O'Rafferty used to live and his wife, Melissa, too.' She gave the address.

There was a short pause broken by the secretary.

'Jaysus, Mary and Joseph! No one's dared to live in that house for nigh on twenty years. Dr Ryan will be able to come and see you but not until three o'clock this afternoon.'

* * *

Alice was still lying flat on her back, staring vacantly at the ceiling, when Dr Ryan, now a white-haired sixty-five year-old, who walked with a pronounced stoop, silently entered the room.

'Mrs Biddle, isn't it? Mrs Alice Biddle?'

'Yes.'

'I'm Dr Ryan. I used to look after the O'Rafferty's. What's the problem?'

Alice turned on her side away from the doctor.

'I hate this house. I want to move out as soon as I can.'

Ryan cleared his throat.

23

'You're in no way ill, Mrs Biddle. This house is known throughout the neighbourhood to be haunted. Some terrible things happened here in Mr O'Rafferty's time. I would suggest that you do one of two things.'

'What?' asked Alice despairingly.

'One is that you pack up and find a similar house to live in.'

'But this is the cheapest in the country.'

Ryan laughed.

'Well, it would be, wouldn't it?'

'Our budget won't manage anything else, I don't think.'

'The second alternative I suggest,' said Ryan 'is that you get a priest to come and exorcize the place. This house does not like being lived in, Mrs Biddle. You should have looked into the question more thoroughly before you came here.'

Alice sat up, supporting herself by her elbows.

'Tell me. What sort of man was Seamus O'Rafferty?'

Ryan went over to the window and looked out. 'It would not be ethical to discuss my previous patients with you,' he replied.

'Was he a good man?'

The doctor turned round facing Alice, his face inexplicably hostile. 'There's good in the worst of us.'

'His wife, Melissa, was she well liked?'

The doctor wiped his forehead with his handkerchief and walked nervously round the room, twisting a lock of hair. 'No, she was not well liked,' he said quietly.

'What did O'Rafferty die of?' asked Alice.

'Cancer,' said Ryan shortly, considering the question to be morbid.

'And Melissa, how did she die?'

'I really don't want to say.'

'Which one died first?' asked Alice, oblivious of Ryan's sudden curtness.

'Melissa went first and Seamus soon after. I attended his funeral. His dog, Mikey, was brought to the cemetery where he was buried. The family wanted Mikey to come along. When the coffin was lowered into the grave, Mikey pulled as hard as he could on his lead and tried to join Mr O'Rafferty. He howled and howled. It was a horrible spectacle to behold.'

'You told me that some terrible things happened in this house,' said Alice. 'What were they?'

'Come now, Mrs Biddle. It's all right to go to confession and absolve yourself but I'm certainly not prepared to endanger my immortal soul by giving this kind of information.'

'I feel better now,' said Alice. Ryan wrote her a prescription for Valium to prevent her from getting anxious again.

Biddle and Mary suddenly came into the room. Dr Ryan put his instruments back into his bag and moved towards the door.

'One other thing,' he said. 'Move into another room. You're sleeping in the room where Mr and Mrs O'Rafferty slept and the room next door is the dressing room where he removed his clothes before going to bed.'

'Did you hear that, Mary?' said Biddle. 'You'll have to move too. You've been so much happier over the last twenty-four hours and we can't have you getting upset again.'

'In no way am I moving,' said Mary. 'I love this room and I've been happier in it than in any bedroom in my life.'

She was bored and restless. She left the room hurriedly as Hannah stood talking to Biddle.

'Where do you think you're going, Mary?' asked Biddle.

'I'm going to look round the house. I'm fascinated by it.'

'You're the only one who is,' said Biddle irritably. 'Hannah, you'd better go with her.'

Mary bounded about like a cat with Hannah following her like a reluctant lady-in-waiting. They came to a narrow corridor, consisting of two bedrooms and a cramped, windowless bathroom. One of the bedrooms had twin beds. Nothing, in the way of ornaments, photographs or cosmetics, had been removed.

Mary went into the room with twin beds, accompanied by her sister. There were peeling posters of male film stars on the walls, with their once virile faces looking cracked and jaundiced. Tooth-cleaning materials lay on a sheet of glass above the washbasin and a tube of contraceptive jelly stood in a mug as if to be hidden. The entire area was covered with cobwebs and dust.

This room had been occupied by Hattie and Biddy O'Rafferty. Some half-finished embroidery lay on one of the bedside tables. On the other lay the complete works of Shakespeare, the collected works of Thomas Hardy and a book about Irish history.

Hattie, an academic and university graduate, had liked to spend her spare time reading. Biddy, who was a professional with a needle and cotton, did embroidery for relaxation and made her own clothes with such expertise that her dresses were often mistaken for designer clothes.

Hannah broke out in a cold sweat. 'For God's sake, let's get out of this room.' Her tone was mixed with fear and irritation.

'Whatever for? It's riveting.'

'Do you mean to tell me that you can't hear it?'

'Hear what?'

'The sound of someone crying and there's so much grief in it, too. It's eerie. I'm getting out of here.'

The twins went into the next door bedroom. In it was an unmade bed with clothes lying on the floor. A portrait of a pensive-looking girl with long, waist-length, red hair and a pointed nose stood on the dressing-table on which cosmetics were strewn, as if their owner had been in a rage or a hurry. The girl in the portrait was Hatty O'Rafferty. She was unsmiling and with her blue eyes lowered, she looked unhappy. This room had belonged to Eileen O'Rafferty, the girl whose beauty had broken the hearts of many a man. The room had a distinctly unpleasant atmosphere in it.

Hannah was about to burst into tears. 'I don't share your morbid fascination for this sort of thing, Mary. Haven't you had enough of it in England? Let's go into the garden.'

'What's the hurry? I want to go up to the attic.'

At the end of the corridor, was a ladder leading to a loft. Mary climbed up it and opened the trap door in the ceiling. Hannah followed her, but only because her father had made her responsible for her.

The first thing Mary found in the loft was a series of upright beams supporting a gabled roof. An equal number of horizontal beams lay on top of them. Mary walked towards an antique, gold-studded pirate's chest with a curved lid in a corner of the loft. On it, also in gold studs, were engraved the initials, S.O'R.

Hannah couldn't get up the ladder. A violent, icy wind forced her to the floor. The strong stench of stale gin, as if on someone's breath, blew into her face. She could feel someone standing by her side, and whoever it was, that person's attitude was distinctly hostile.

'Mary, for God's sake come down!'

This was all she could say. The being standing by her side was driving her downstairs. She rolled down the steep staircase like an India rubber ball and screamed for her father who didn't answer. She rushed out into the garden.

Mary wondered whether the chest was locked but it opened effortlessly. It contained an endless number of handwritten letters, photographs and portraits. The first picture she saw was one of an unusually handsome man in his fifties, with grey eyes and thick, black hair with a small lock falling over his forehead. His white shirt was open at the neck, showing a broad, tanned chest. She knew who he was because she had seen him in her dream. She couldn't take her eyes away from the picture and her heart hammered against her ribs. She had fallen in love with the late Seamus O'Rafferty and the late Seamus O'Rafferty had fallen in love with her.

Then she discovered a paper-opening knife with an engraving on it, reading, 'To Uncle Seamus, with love from Sarah'. Being psychic, if only to some extent, Mary immediately linked the knife to the linoleum-floored corridor. This would have terrified most people but it fascinated Mary.

She heard her father's voice from below. 'If you don't come down from there at once, I'm coming up to get you.'

'It's no good. I'm staying.'

'Didn't you hear me, you silly little fool?' shouted Biddle. 'Come out of there this instant.'

Mary seemed drugged.

'No, I belong up here. I'm staying here for ever.'

Biddle lost his temper.

'I thought I told you to come down. I will not be disobeyed! Do you realize how dangerous it is up there, particularly at night?'

Mary ignored her father. Biddle was enraged because he wasn't fit enough to climb up and down ladders easily. He reached the top of the ladder, exhausted, and tried to climb through the trap door.

He was suddenly hit by a violent and malevolent draught.

'Mary, for God's sake help me!'

His grip on the rungs of the ladder weakened. He fell to the floor and broke his neck.

Part II

O'Rafferty and Sarah

The year was 1975. Sarah Lloyd was the youngest of the four children of Sir Alec Lloyd, a newspaper proprietor in London. Her mother, Lady Tessa Lloyd, entertained lavishly to promote her husband's trade. Sir Alec was the oldest of a family of seven children, Charles, James, Frank, Jenny, Julia and Melissa, the youngest.

The children, with the exception of Melissa, who was spoiled relentlessly by her father, had a puritanical and rigidly strict upbringing. They were forced to adhere to the work ethic and were punished when their school grades were poor.

Their father, Selwyn, a self-made millionaire and his brother, Dyfed, hailed from South Wales. Selwyn was a workaholic who set up the family business in London. He and his wife were bitterly opposed to Melissa marrying a swarthy, fierce-tempered, rough diamond of an Irishman, who was known to have punched his caretaker in the jaw in his teens, knocking out his false teeth, because the caretaker didn't recognize him when he said he had lost his key.

Melissa was hopelessly in love with O'Rafferty and settled in Ireland where she had six children. Her oldest daughter, Biddy, had dark hair, fresh features, a serious countenance and was beautiful in an austere, Victorian sort of way. She was twenty.

Hattie, aged nineteen, had wavy, red hair growing to her waist. She had striking, pre-Raphaelite colouring, was highly articulate and could be quite fiery when her path was crossed.

Eileen, aged eighteen, was graced with phenomenally good looks. Her gypsy-like, black, layered hair and enormous, grey eyes caused men to chase her in droves. She was the twin sister of Shamie who shared her features but, as a boy, he was less striking to look at.

Sean, aged sixteen, was the most sensitive and nervy of his siblings. He was better-looking than his brothers, bearing an uncanny, facial resemblance to his father whose temper terrified him. Sean's jumpy disposition progressed to episodes of intermittent insecurity. Women chased him just as men chased his sisters. He later had a series of affairs, many of which were short-lived, because women had an overbearing effect on him which reminded him of his father.

Paddy, the youngest and his parents' favourite, was wild and exceptionally naughty. He was eight years old. He infuriated his over-disciplined siblings who locked him in the bathroom every time he misbehaved.

'Have you got any sisters, Paddy, dear?' his schoolteacher asked him.

'Three, sir.'

'Is that so, now? What are they like?'

'Bloody sexy, sir.'

* * *

Sarah Lloyd was nineteen. She had invited Hattie to stay for the Easter holidays in her family's villa in the South of France. It was breezy and Sarah's eldest brother, Selwyn, took Hattie sailing. Her red hair was arranged in a pony-tail and she wore blue-lensed sunglasses to match her sweater. The boom swung straight in her face, shattering pieces of glass in her eye. Sarah's mother Tessa took

Hattie to hospital where she had to wait for three hours in casualty before being seen. The whole episode irritated the older woman who thought it showed a lack of common sense to wear sunglasses on a sailing boat.

The summer passed by quickly. Tessa had organized a number of soirées for her husband in their elegant London house which was permanently thronged with journalists and editors. Tessa was exhausted. July came. She went into Sarah's room one morning.

'Sarah, darling, I'm afraid we've got to move you out of here in August because I'm having your room redecorated. The men will be starting work at the beginning of the month.'

'Where will I go?' asked Sarah.

'What do you mean – where will you go? We had Hattie O'Rafferty to stay for the whole of the Easter holidays. Why don't you ring up your Aunt Melissa and ask her very politely if it would be all right for you to stay in her house in Ireland for a few weeks.'

'But I can't ring someone up, asking myself to their house for so long!'

'Hullo. This is Sarah Lloyd. May I speak to my Aunt Melissa, please?'

A maid had taken the call.

'You want to speak to Mrs O'Rafferty? She won't be long.'

'Aunt Melissa?'

'Yes. Who's that?'

'It's Sarah, Sarah Lloyd. My mother has turned me out of my room because she's redecorating it. She says I can't stay at home for the whole of August.'

Melissa took a swig of gin. (It was nine-thirty a.m.)

'Well, you're welcome to come and stay with us. I can't say you'll find it very exciting. It will be just Seamus, the children and I.'

Sarah felt relieved.

'That really is terribly kind of you. What day would suit you?'

'Come whenever you like, Sarah, and stay till your mother's finished having your room done up.'

* * *

Sarah drove to the O'Rafferty's in a black Mini Clubman Estate which looked like a miniature hearse. She crossed the water on a bumpy ferry, on which a lot of the passengers were sick. Her map-reading skills were poor and although she managed to find the right area, she couldn't find Mulligan Manor.

She had been driving backwards and forwards along the same road for an hour and had to make an effort not to burst into tears. She pulled into the side and got out. It took her half an hour to cross the fields and reach the nearest cottage. It was a tiny place with weather-worn, stone walls, windows the size of ashtrays and a thatched roof.

Sarah knew a little Irish history and feared those natives she had never met. She knocked timidly on the door which was opened by an old woman with a black shawl covering most of her face. Sarah automatically assumed she was a widow.

'Good afternoon. I'm sorry to trouble you. Do you by any chance know the way to Mulligan Manor where Mr O'Rafferty lives?'

The woman looked Sarah up and down. She observed her honey-coloured pony-tail with blonde streaks and her hanging gold ear-rings. The woman objected to Sarah's array of gold necklaces most of all. She continued to stare at Sarah, her small, black eyes showing neither warmth nor a desire to help.

'I'm sorry I intruded on you. I didn't mean to disturb you. I'm lost you see.'

Without warning, the woman embarked on a hackneyed imitation of Sarah's English accent before returning to her husky, Irish brogue.

'It's cottages such as mine that your fellow countrymen burnt down, slaying innocent babies in their beds.'

'That's not my fault. I wasn't even alive.'

'Your kind's not wanted here. Why don't you go back to London?'

'Why don't you shove a lighted match up your arse, you potty, old crone?'

The door was slammed in her face. Sarah, walked on, feeling frustrated and dejected. She decided that she would use an Irish accent when she came to the next house. She picked up her car and continued for two miles until she found another cottage.

A similarly dressed woman to the last one opened the door. Sarah wondered if a black shawl was some sort of uniform. She broke into a bogus, Irish brogue.

The woman was pleasant and sympathetic.

'There's Mulligan Manor,' she said, pointing to a rambling, white house at the top of a hill. 'Wait one minute, dear. I've just made some buns. I'd like you to have one.'

Sarah thanked the woman profusely, keeping up her Irish accent.

'Would you like to come inside, dear?'

Sarah grew suspicious. She feared that her accent had sounded false and thought that the woman would try to harm her in some way. The woman, who introduced herself as Shelagh, beckoned her to a dwindling fire. The buns she had cooked were by the grate. Shelagh passed a plate of buns to Sarah and ate one herself.

'So where are you from, young lady?'

'Me? I was born in Dublin,' Sarah lied. 'I've come to see the O'Rafferty's. Have you lived here all your life?'

'That, I have. You may not know this but I used to be

the nanny to all the O'Rafferty children. They still come and see me.'

'I didn't know that but I must be getting on. Thank you so much for the bun.' Sarah only realized after she had spoken that she had returned to her clipped, English rasp.

Shelagh waved goodbye, not without a perplexed expression on her face, and Sarah shook her hand. 'Enjoy your stay with the O'Rafferty's,' she said kindly.

Sarah drove up the steep hill to Mulligan Manor and as she came closer, she became aware of the size of the large, white house which looked imposingly onto the windswept valley.

A blistering blockbuster of a row had been taking place in the house for over half an hour. O'Rafferty was bellowing at two of his daughters, Hattie and Biddy, and accusing them of what he called their 'disgusting bad manners', because they had told their mother that her excessive drinking was damaging her liver as well as the lives of her children.

O'Rafferty was in his fifties. He was leaning out of an open window overlooking the drive, wearing a white shirt with most of its buttons undone, accentuating his broad, bronzed chest.

'It's not only your foul, dastardly insolence towards your mother that I'm complaining about,' he screamed, and Sarah feared that he might break his vocal cords at any moment. 'I found contraceptives in your room today. No one would have thought that I'd brought you up as decent Catholics.'

'Why do you have to treat us like children?' asked Biddy, her voice raised to the same pitch as her father's.

O'Rafferty took the contraceptive pills out of their packets and threw them out of the window. Sarah was just pulling up and felt them land on the front of her car. Astounded, she got out and picked up four strips of Minovlar ED which had fallen to the ground. She put them in her pocket. She got back into her car and was about to park in the corner of the drive, thinking that this was a dream. She heard the continued shouts of the same man with a rasping Dublin accent.

'If you don't get your fat asses out of this house by the time I get back from the races, I'll pick yer both up by the hair and fling yer both out of the bleedin' window.'

A pink suitcase with its contents falling out landed on the front of Sarah's car. A beige suitcase with books spilling out of it followed in its wake.

Sarah wondered what she should do next. She got out of the car and put the things back in the suitcases and closed them. Then she carried them to the front door where she left them. She lifted her own suitcase, which was black and shiny with S.L. engraved on it in heavy, gold letters, and walked, not without some apprehension, into the house.

The front door was ajar and she strode straight in, dreading what might be awaiting her inside. She saw no sign of Hattie or Biddy who had left through another exit. They found their suitcases, got into Biddy's car and headed for Dublin. Undaunted by their father's fury, they checked into the most luxurious and expensive hotel in the city where he had an account. With broad smiles on their faces, they went to the reception desk.

'My name's Biddy O'Rafferty and this is my sister, Hattie. Our father, Mr Seamus O'Rafferty, has an account here. Unfortunately, his house is being renovated at the moment and he told us to clock in here for a few weeks. We'd be grateful for a suite each. Being the elder sister, I would like the suite that the Burtons stayed in when they came to Dublin.'

The hotel manager was called O'Grady. He was a small

man with a black, goatee beard. He told the girls that two separate suites were available.

'Just send the bill to Mr O'Rafferty, if you would. Right, Hat?'

'Right, Bid.'

* * *

Once inside the house, Sarah heard more ferocious shouting. O'Rafferty was upstairs in his son Sean's bedroom.

'Would you get the hell out of that bed, you idle brat! Why didn't you go to mass this morning?'

'Because the wine's so sour and you always insist on us drinking it,' replied Sean quietly.

O'Rafferty dragged Sean from his bed and gave him a resounding slap on the ear. Eileen, one of O'Rafferty's daughters, rushed into the room, but her father was in such a temper that he didn't see her.

'I will not tolerate such repulsive and damnable blasphemy being uttered under my roof!' shouted O'Rafferty. He began to shake Sean like a rag doll, terrifying him.

Eileen went up to her father and pointed her finger at him, her eyes screwed up with rage.

'Don't you dare so much as lay another finger on that boy! Leave him alone, you bully.'

'Would you mind your own business, you stupid woman!'

'My brother's pain is every bit my business.'

O'Rafferty slapped his daughter across the face but not as hard as he had hit Sean. Eileen kicked her father in the private parts, as hard as she could. He let out a high-pitched scream and rolled down the stairs where he curled up in a ball, writhing with pain.

As the pain began to lessen, O'Rafferty heard footsteps. He saw a garishly-dressed, young woman standing over him.

'Uncle Seamus? Are you all right?'

'You've got an educated English voice. Who are you?' asked O'Rafferty, his voice scarcely above a whisper.

'My name's Sarah Lloyd. I'm your niece. Aunt Melissa is my father's youngest sister.'

'Is that so, now? Welcome to Mulligan Manor.'

'Don't you remember me, Uncle Seamus?' asked Sarah, who felt rather hurt. 'You must remember me. You used to bribe me with half a crown to sing Irish rebel songs outside Brigadier Hamlyn-Williams's room at seven o'clock in the morning, when we were all staying in my Uncle Charles's house.'

A friendly smile came on to O'Rafferty's face. He staggered to his feet and Sarah held his arm.

'So you were that dear little girl. You could never remember the words of the songs, so I had to write them out for you in capitals. Do you remember when the Brigadier leapt out of bed and came to the door, hiding his nakedness with a coat showing a sea of medals, won for serving the British Empire?' asked O'Rafferty, adding, 'So you've travelled all these miles to visit your poor Uncle Seamus? I must say I call that really handsome of you. Let's go to my study. You'll need a strong drink after all this travelling and noise. I think you heard an argument didn't you?'

'Well, I heard voices raised in anger but I didn't hear any words.'

'I want you to know how much I love all my children, although I shout at them. They get a bit naughty sometimes. I'm not the monster you may think I am.'

O'Rafferty helped Sarah to take off her leopard-skin coat.

'Sure, 'tis a mighty, fancy coat you've got,' he said.

'Well, it's really very old. It used to belong to my mother,' replied Sarah demurely.

O'Rafferty handled the coat delicately, as if it were china, and hung it up in a cupboard in the hall.

'Come on into the study, old girl. You could be doing with a drink after your long journey all these miles to see your dotty Uncle Seamus.'

He ushered her into a small, spartan room overlooking a lawn, containing two armchairs that needed re-covering, a big, leather-topped desk with mounds of papers on it and a grey switchboard on a shelf above it, next to an anglepoise lamp.

He put his hand on her shoulder and took her over to the drinks tray.

'Well, Sarah, what will you have?'

She had already developed an animal attraction towards this man and became desperately shy. She fought to find her words.

'Would it be awfully outrageous if I had some whisky, Uncle Seamus?'

'Sure, it wouldn't. Everyone likes a different amount. Do you mind helping yourself?'

Sarah hoped that the whisky would drown her shyness and replace it with pleasure to be in the company of this fiery man with his rugged good looks. She turned away from her uncle and poured herself a glass of neat whisky and drank a huge gulp from it, standing by his side. He poured himself the same drink, diluted it with soda and ice and gave Sarah some more, noticing that her glass was nearly empty.

They sat down in the two facing armchairs and drank in a silence, broken eventually by Sarah whose instant shedding of her inhibitions and sudden onset of violent lust for her uncle terrified her. She was afraid that she would lose control and rush over to him and throw herself at him.

'Uncle Seamus?'

'Yes, my dear?'

'I – er – I never had the faintest idea that you were so good-looking.'

O'Rafferty slapped his thigh and laughed. 'Well, if that isn't a rare compliment indeed! You'd have had frailer men than me blushing through what you said.'

'May I have another drink please?' Sarah asked, still with a remnant of shyness in her voice which he found charming. 'I don't normally drink like this but this is a special occasion.'

O'Rafferty refilled her glass and sat with one leg crossed at right angles over the other. The grey trousers he wore were tight-fitting and the position he sat in accentuated his virility. Sarah couldn't trust herself to look.

O'Rafferty had nearly finished his whisky and soda.

'Your smart, blue trousers, matching shirt and the gold jewellery – did those belong to your mother too?'

Sarah was too intoxicated to brood about whether he was teasing her or flattering her. 'Why, no. I bought them in London. Not all my wardrobe consists of my mother's clothes.'

O'Rafferty laughed again. He liked Sarah's cockiness and her quick tongue, alternating unpredictably with girlish modesty.

'Well then, Sarah, my pretty, little niece, can you sing me one of them rebel songs that you sang outside Brigadier Hamlyn-Williams's door at seven o'clock in the morning?'

'What about *The Old Alarum Clock*?' suggested Sarah.

O'Rafferty laughed.

'That's a saucy song, isn't it b'Jaysus?'

He was right. The black-humoured song was about an IRA volunteer who had been arrested on an explosives charge. It had an extremely provocative chorus repeating the words, '*Ah, me coople of sticks of gelig-i-nite and me old alarum clock.*' Sarah was about to sing it when the telephone rang. O'Rafferty was irritated at having his conversation with such a delightful companion interrupted. He swore under his breath and went over to the switchboard. He picked up the phone.

'O'Rafferty.'

'Oh, Mr O'Rafferty. Sure, I'm so sorry to trouble you in this way. This is O'Grady, the manager of the Rockefeller Plaza Hotel in Dublin.'

'Yes? What is it?'

O'Grady paused to find his words. He had considered O'Rafferty to be a man who made an awful lot of noise and was in awe of him.

'It's about Miss Hattie and Miss Biddy, sir. Sure, 'tis no more than a formality. They came here and said that their rooms were being redecorated and that you had sent them here. You'll be pleased to hear that I've managed to put Miss Biddy in the suite Elizabeth Taylor and Richard Burton used when they came to Dublin. I've put Miss Hattie up in an equally luxurious and comfortable suite overlooking the Post Office where the Great Rebellion started. They said that you had told them to stay for a few weeks and it's a rare honour to have them here, sir. I do hope this meets with your approval.'

O'Rafferty felt as if someone had shot him in the foot. The rage which surged through him was so hideous and violent that he was lost for words. Eventually, he came out of verbal deadlock. He bellowed at length and because Sarah was not involved, she enjoyed every minute of it. Eventually, O'Rafferty began to tire. His throat became sore and his voice husky.

'Mr O'Grady, would you please send them home this instant? I gave them no authority whatever to book into your hotel.'

O'Grady wiped his sweating forehead with his handkerchief. His hand shook as he held the receiver a yard away from his ear. O'Rafferty had been one of his

40

most regular clients and, apart from his awesome temper, he was afraid of losing his custom.

'I really do apologize, sir. I had no idea. I will alert them and send them home immediately.' O'Grady took a swig of brandy which he kept under the reception desk. 'Sure, I'm sorry to have to mention this, sir. There's just a small question of payment.'

'Payment? B'Jaysus, Mr O'Grady, are you trying to give me a heart attack?'

'Sure, it costs three hundred pounds a night to stay in the Taylor and Burton suite. Miss Biddy has been there for half an hour already, so you will have to be charged. I tried to contact you earlier but your line was engaged.'

O'Rafferty felt rage simmering again but struggled to control it so as not to upset Sarah.

O'Grady continued, his voice scarcely above a whisper. 'There is of course, an additional charge.'

'For Christ's sake, speak up, Mr O'Grady!'

'Sorry, sir. I was talking about the additional charges. Miss Biddy has been entertaining a number of young gentlemen from Trinity College. Caviar, lobster and champagne were ordered, sir. Two of the gentlemen stayed so I was obliged to charge them too. Apparently, the three had one mother of a time, if you'll pardon the ribaldry, sir.'

'Get Biddy on the line!' shouted O'Rafferty.

'Yes, sir.'

A pause ensued. O'Rafferty picked up a heavy ashtray and was about to throw it through a window.

'Sure, I'm ever so sorry, sir. Miss Biddy's left her phone off the hook. She must be resting after her energy expenditure, begging your pardon, sir.'

* * *

The erring sisters decided not to go home straight away. One meal, namely dinner, was sufficient to face their father's wrath. They had a boozy lunch in Dublin and went home later when they knew that he would be resting. They had bought expensive dresses and shoes, using their overdrafts.

They had stiff drinks in the living room in the house they called 'Hangover Hall', alternating with 'Cold Comfort Farm', depending on which parent their bitterness was directed towards at the time. They heard their father's heavy footsteps as he came down the stairs. They remained as calm as possible, sitting on a sofa, in their pretty, new dresses.

Sarah didn't want to be in the room while O'Rafferty's wrath erupted against his daughters. As he strode into the living room, she hid in the dining room and listened at the door.

'Get the hell off your backsides and go straight to my study!'

The sisters obeyed. Once the study door was closed, Sarah listened outside. Even through the thick, wooden door, O'Rafferty's shouts hurt her ears so she shielded them, allowing enough leeway to hear his words.

'How dare you even think of booking into the two most expensive suites in the Rockefeller?' came the booming voice and even the thick, oak walls vibrated.

'What were we expected to do?' asked Biddy who had fractionally more courage than Hattie.

O'Rafferty dragged them to the fender. He spanked their bottoms, shouting as he did so.

'When I throw you out of the house because of your disgusting references to your mother's problem, by Jaysus, you clock into the YWCA and say your prayers!'

Hattie was weeping by now but Biddy was holding steady.

'Don't you understand, Da?' she said. 'This problem is going to affect you one day, not just us. Her liver will crack up and you'll be alone.'

'The problem is a matter between me and her!' shouted O'Rafferty. 'It's nothing whatever to do with you. It's none of your goddamn business, do you hear?'

* * *

The whole family were there for dinner that evening. Just before dinner, Melissa rushed to the drinks tray in the living room, knelt surreptitiously on the floor and hurriedly drank some gin out of the bottle. She lifted her dress and hid the bottle in her roll-on. When she got up, she saw Sarah standing in front of her.

'Aunt Melissa?' ventured the dumbfounded girl.

'Oh, yes, Sarah. It is Sarah, isn't it?' said Melissa, slurring her words.

'Yes. It's awfully sweet of you to have me to stay.'

'You can come whenever you want. As you probably know, Seamus is awfully fond of you. I wish you'd come more often.'

As Melissa spoke, the bottle of gin fell to the floor. She picked it up and carried it under her arm, hopefully assuming that her gesture would go unnoticed.

Sarah sat next to O'Rafferty at dinner. Eileen, Hattie and Biddy sat at the same side of the table with eight-year-old Paddy sitting between them. Paddy was still quite small and only his head and shoulders could be seen, which melted his father's heart.

On the opposite side sat Sean and Shamie. Sean kept dropping things throughout the meal because of his ingrained, nervous temperament. Shamie compensated for these failings with a superb sense of humour and spontaneous laughter at Sarah's jokes.

Melissa sat in her usual place, keeping her bottle of gin under her chair. She bent down to drink from it even more frequently than she had done at previous meals.

'Hullo, little Mikey. How about a nice piece of meat for you, Mikey?' she said.

As well as being nervy, Sean was in a bad mood that evening because of a girl.

'Mikey's over here, Mummy,' he said aggressively. 'He's lying down behind my chair.'

Melissa saw that there was no point in keeping the bottle of gin on the floor. She put it on the table by her glass. Every time she poured the gin into the glass, the eyes of Eileen, Hattie and Biddy would follow the bottle from the glass back to the table. Each time she raised the glass to her lips, the eyes of the three girls would follow the glass as it was raised and then put back on the table.

Shamie was giggling helplessly and Sarah was busy making O'Rafferty laugh. He soon knew what was happening.

'Eileen, Hattie and Biddy, if I see yet a further display of your disgusting, bad manners, I'll take you outside and spank your bottoms, as big as you are!'

Chocolate mousse was brought to the table. Sarah was served first but she was on a diet and took very little.

'Come on, Sarah, you can do better than that. That looks like something out of a flaming dog's arse!' said O'Rafferty.

'I've had so much of the delicious, first course, I haven't got any room, Uncle Seamus.'

The children passed a jug of cream in a saucer round the table. Paddy was clumsy after helping himself and accidentally let the jug fall onto Hattie's dress.

'For God's sake, Paddy, can't you look what you're doing?'

'Knock it off, Hattie!' bawled O'Rafferty. 'You were eight once.'

Hattie lowered her wavy, red head and her silent tears

rolled down her cheeks unchecked. Biddy looked briefly at her sister and glared at her father, white with rage.

'When we were eight, we weren't spoiled like that little brat. The children I look after in my job are all younger than him and you should see their good manners!' she shouted.

'What he needs is a good kick in the pants,' said Sean.

'He needs far more than a kick in the pants!' shouted Biddy. 'He needs a bloody, good thrashing – the selfish, little lout. Not only that, he didn't even say "sorry".'

Sarah got a certain amount of enjoyment out of a row which didn't concern her but on this occasion she felt awkward. She began to stack up the plates.

O'Rafferty blew up yet again.

'I will not tolerate my daughters sitting on their backsides while my guest, Sarah, is left to clear the table!'

'Oh, it's all right,' said Sarah, who had been strictly disciplined to clear tables in the houses in which she was a guest.

Suddenly, she caught Biddy's eye. Her cousin's was a look that made her tremble with fear. She sat down and stared at her hands. She wished the meal would end. She was no longer amused by her uncle's wrath and her aunt's drunkenness. She waited for her cousins to clear the table. When they had finished, she walked out of the room with her hands clasped in front of her and her head lowered.

* * *

It was breakfast time the following morning. O'Rafferty suddenly stopped eating. He and Sarah were alone.

'Sarah?'

'Yes, Uncle Seamus.'

'Sarah, my pretty, little niece?'

She looked up abruptly, her mouth full of toast which

45

she swallowed hurriedly. She saw her uncle looking at her.

'Will you come and have a drink with me in my study at six o'clock this evening?'

'Yes, of course. Do I get an honorary spanking to go with it?'

O'Rafferty laughed loudly, relieved that Sarah had accepted his invitation. He sat back in his chair, wallowing like a satiated cat.

Sarah went to her room before the rest of the family came down. She made her bed and went into the living room to read her book, unable to concentrate, thinking about what was going to happen in her uncle's study.

* * *

O'Rafferty had a passion for racing and owned a large number of racehorses. He was in an ebullient mood that day, due to the acquisition of a new horse which he called Britbuster, a restless, black creature with a white star between his eyes. The horse seemed uncontrollable and spent his first day on O'Rafferty's hands kicking the stable door.

Sarah put on a pale blue, cotton dress which she covered with a leopard-skin shawl. She wore pale blue shoes with white, fishnet tights and splashed herself with Chanel Number 5. She loosened her hair and let it fall over her shoulders.

O'Rafferty was waiting for her in his study, chain smoking. He had one leg crossed at right angles over the other, a pose which Sarah had seen before and it excited her. He had on black trousers, a clean, white shirt with the two top buttons undone and a greyish tie loosened at the neck. This excited her even more.

O'Rafferty was the first to break the silence.

'So you came, my pretty, little niece. With your lovely,

blue eyes matching your dress and shoes, you look fit to kill any man in the neighbourhood. You could do with a drink. What will you have?'

Sarah went over to where the drinks were kept and asked with uncharacteristic timidity if she could have some whisky.

O'Rafferty handed her one of the many whisky bottles. She noticed long lines of lipstick at the back of the bottle, two of them at least an inch apart. As if ashamed, O'Rafferty turned the bottle round so that its label was facing him. There was a fleeting look of sadness in his eyes. He poured whisky and soda into a glass for himself.

'Help yourself, Sarah. Only you know how you want it.'

Sarah felt that she was losing her nerve and poured herself three quarters of a glass of neat whisky. She drained half of it, turning away from her uncle.

'I didn't know you were so thirsty.' He poured more whisky into her glass. 'You shouldn't overdo it, Sarah. Otherwise, you'll spoil things. Just take a little at a time.'

Sarah sat down opposite O'Rafferty and crossed her fishnet-covered legs. The whisky had drowned her shyness and emboldened her.

'I hope I'm not going to be tempted to be naughty, Uncle Seamus.'

He ignored her remark and smiled.

'Can you dance, my pretty, little niece?'

'Yes, provided I'm loaded.'

'Loaded with what?'

'Booze.'

O'Rafferty laughed and swallowed a few mouthfuls of his whisky and soda. He pointed to an old-fashioned tape recorder on a table by his chair. He turned it on and continued to stare at her. The machine began to play Irish rebel songs, robustly sung by the *Dubliners*. Sarah had sung many of these songs outside Brigadier Hamlyn-

47

Williams's room at seven o'clock in the morning as a child at O'Rafferty's request.

God Save Ireland, say the Heroes, a stirring, fast-moving song, repeating the words, *If it's on the scaffold high or the battlefield we die,* flooded the room as the whisky surged through Sarah's blood. She looked at her uncle and he looked at her.

'Dance, Sarah, my pretty, little niece! Hurl fire into a man's heart from your lovely face.'

Sarah kicked off her shoes and removed her leopard-skin shawl, waving it from one side to the other and staring at her uncle's animated eyes throughout.

'Wait,' said O'Rafferty.

He went to his desk drawer and produced a rolled-up, republican flag. He threw it to Sarah. 'Use this instead of the shawl.'

Sarah was drunk by now. She obeyed her uncle and danced well, her style a cross between Flamenco and Israeli. O'Rafferty clapped in time to the music.

Sarah was very unfit and soon became exhausted. She sat on the floor, leaning backwards on her hands. She waited to regain her breath and rose to her feet.

O'Rafferty turned the machine off and stood up. He lowered the blinds and locked the door. Then he walked over to Sarah.

'My God, Sarah, what have you done to me? I've never met the like of this before.'

He kissed her on the mouth, feeling his way round her teeth with his tongue. He was struck by the sweetness of her breath. He ran his hands through her hair and licked her face and ears.

'Uncle Seamus, do you think this is fair on Aunt Melissa?'

'Sure it's fair. You can be in love with two people at once, can't you?'

Suddenly, O'Rafferty remembered an occasion when he

48

and Melissa were first married. Melissa had had an affair with a horse trainer called Tom Delaney. O'Rafferty had found them up to no good in the back of Delaney's car. He had wrenched the door open, dragged his rival out by the scruff of his neck and had savagely beaten him up.

'You can be in love with two people at once, can't you?' Melissa had said.

A sad, brooding look clouded over O'Rafferty's face. Then he kissed his niece again, failing to notice the handle of the door turning.

'What's going on, Seamus? I want to come in.'

O'Rafferty raised the blinds and went over to unlock the door as Sarah put on her shoes and shawl and straightened her hair. She rolled up the flag and put it back in the drawer.

Melissa was outside, wearing a dressing-gown and looking bleary-eyed and low-spirited, as she normally did, following a deep sleep in the afternoon.

'Why did you lock me out, Seamus?'

'Because I don't want you drinking too early before dinner. It's not good for you.'

'I'm over twenty-one and I'll do what I want.'

'All right, all right. I suppose I can't stop you. It's your health you're ruining, not mine.'

Melissa looked vacantly round the room and noticed Sarah who was standing by the window.

'Hullo, Sarah, dear, I didn't see you.'

Sarah went over to her aunt and kissed her on both cheeks.

'Good-evening, Aunt Melissa,' she said with undisguised awkwardness. 'Isn't it a splendid sunset?'

'Has Seamus shown you the new horse? He's magnificent.'

'Not yet. I'd like to see him.'

'Well, that's settled then,' said O'Rafferty, a little nervous

49

in the company of the two women. 'I'll show him to you after dinner.'

Sarah sat next to Melissa at dinner and delighted her by telling her funny stories, her guilt and embarrassment washed away by drink.

Hattie and Biddy were shouting across the table at Eileen's twin brother, Shamie, accusing him in a non-specific manner, of generalized cowardice and unquestioning subservience towards his parents.

Sean waded into the conversation between his siblings. He wasn't interested in whether or not Shamie obeyed his parents, because his fifteen-year-old girlfriend, Lilly, had been flirting with a boy older than he. He lunged at Hattie and Biddy.

'You're such fockin' bores, both of you! Can't you ever talk about anything else?'

'You spoilt, disloyal, little brat!' shouted Biddy. 'Don't expect either of us to stick up for you again.'

'You're not still upset about Lilly, are you?' asked Eileen. 'Besides, I saw you dancing with Michelle, cheek to cheek, last night.'

Pandemonium, almost on a par with the bickering over state sovereignty before the First World War, dominated the dinner. O'Rafferty banged the table and shouted at his children, threatening to turn them all out of the house unless they stopped quarrelling. Melissa continued to pump herself with gin from the bottle under the table, while Sarah chatted nervously to her.

Melissa drank because she had no need to work. From the time she got up in the morning until the time she went to bed, she had nothing to do and, because Irish life had fossilized her, as is the case with many English women who settle in Ireland, she no longer had the imagination to set herself a constructive, occupational project.

50

O'Rafferty loved her uncompromisingly and put himself out to make her life as enjoyable as possible. He asked her once if living in the country was making her unhappy but she denied this and turned down his offer to move somewhere less remote.

O'Rafferty got up every morning at five o'clock to attend to the farm and returned to the house just before lunch. Melissa woke up between nine and ten o'clock each day, dressed and went straight to the drinks tray and drank a substantial amount of gin before lunch.

To look at, she was not an unattractive woman but she saw herself as ageing. She began to resent the fresh, good looks of her daughters who had inherited her skin colouring and bone structure. Her resentment deteriorated to overt antagonism which descended to displays of blatant hostility.

When Hattie was thirteen, Melissa had confided in her about her uncontrollable addiction to alcohol. Hattie was pleasant and sympathetic but Melissa suddenly turned on her and Hattie's protective attitude towards her mother soon turned to loathing, shown in the form of adolescent sullenness.

Even beneath the blanket of gin, Melissa was sharply sensitive to dumb insolence. Her immediate reaction would be to go crying to her husband, saying that Hattie had been rude and vicious without cause. O'Rafferty's feelings for his wife were blind, passionate and adoring and even when she was at fault, he could see no wrong in her. He would punish Hattie and any other of her siblings who fell into the same trap.

The ones who despised Melissa most were Hattie and Biddy. For some reason, Eileen hated her mother less than her sisters, possibly because they were very close so she tended to keep herself aloof from them.

When Hattie was in her teens, she fell in love with a boy two years her senior called Jeff. She waited for two

51

weeks for him to ring her up to ask her out. Finally, he rang. Melissa, as was always the case, had very little to do and listened in on the line.

'Look, I'm sorry, Hat. I know you're not a bad lay but I'm not happy about us. We've got nothing in common. We don't have the same interests and we're just not compatible.'

'Do you mean you don't want to see me again?'

'Sorry, Hat, that's just about it. Maybe it's something to do with me.'

'But Jeff...'

'I don't want to talk about it any more. It's over.'

He hung up.

Hattie rushed to the room she shared with Biddy and locked the door. She sobbed for an hour. Then she washed and dried her face and went to find her sister.

Melissa was sitting at the end of the corridor, blocking her path, her eyes bloodshot. She was smiling and what confused Hattie most of all, was the fact that she didn't know whether it was a smile of support or disdain. Her speech was slurred.

'We all get crossed in love, dear. Don't kid yourself that you're unique because you're not.'

Melissa never remembered the things that she had said when she'd been drinking, so her conscience was seldom active. Her intelligence remained intact but her memory, both long and short term, was poor. She felt that Hattie and Biddy were her worst enemies. She never remembered occasions when they had been kind to her and despised them both.

She turned to Sarah who was smiling angelically at her. Her hair had been carefully brushed and arranged in a plait, secured by blue ribbon to match her dress.

'Tell me, Sarah, are there ever ghastly rows like this in your family?'

Sarah was so preoccupied with her uncle that she had no wish to get involved in these fiery arguments. All she wanted was to be at peace with everyone at the table. She was unaware of Melissa's conduct towards her daughters and felt sorry for her because she was an alcoholic. She hardly knew her aunt and was confused by Hattie's and Biddy's stories.

'Good God, Aunt Melissa, in comparison with the rows at home, the bickerings at this table are nothing. Do you know that I came down to breakfast one morning and found blood in the butter?'

Melissa felt at ease with Sarah whose sense of humour relieved her drink-sodden anxiety.

'Whose blood was it and how was it shed?' she asked, her speech slurred.

'Oh, it was my brother's, I think. My sister rushed at him with a carving knife because he took *The News of the World* out of her hand when she was reading it. It was at the time of the Profumo affair.

'There was another time when my brother and sister quarrelled because my brother didn't want to play tennis with my sister. She threw a bottle of ink at him and it went all over the drapes. My mother locked them both in a room and made them act a scene from *Romeo and Juliet*. You should have heard them acting the speech beginning: "*Good pilgrim, you do wrong your hand too much*".'

Sarah recited the short speech, speaking the words of passionate love with the mimicked rage of her sister. Melissa laughed until her face was wet with tears.

'It's a pleasure having you here, Sarah. You're a really good guest.'

'Well, I can but try, Aunt Melissa. I wouldn't be much fun if I were a bad guest.'

As she spoke, a surge of violent anxiety, accompanied by depression, stormed through Sarah, caused by her betrayal of her aunt. She came out in a cold, shaking sweat and hyperventilated. She knew that the only thing that could shake off the panic attack would be a massive swig of gin.

'Aunt Melissa, I think I've got an asthma attack. Would you mind terribly if I were to have a glass of your – er – that beverage you keep under the table?'

Melissa frosted over. She failed to grant Sarah's request and went into a strange trance. Sarah had no idea whether it was hostile or melancholic. Biddy, who had heard everything, caught Sarah's eye and got the giggles.

O'Rafferty, at the other end of the table, had heard nothing of Sarah's and Melissa's conversation. He leant over to Paddy who was sitting next to him and whispered in his ear.

'Paddy, dear, Eileen's not wearing any shoes or socks. Get under the table and tickle her toes.'

Paddy obeyed and Eileen let out a short scream. O'Rafferty got the giggles.

'I thought you were all going to the cinema in Dublin tonight,' he said, still in good spirits. 'If you're going, you'd better go now.'

'It's *Gentlemen Prefer Blondes* you're going to see, isn't it?' asked Melissa.

'No,' said Sean, rather rudely, *Some Like It Hot*.

'Are you going, Sarah?'

'No, I'll stay here. I've seen the film at least ten times.'

'Oh, of course, I forgot. Seamus is going to show you Britbuster tonight, isn't he?'

'Yes, he is. I'd much rather see the horse than *Some Like It Hot*.'

* * *

It had started to rain. O'Rafferty and Sarah walked along a gravelly path to the stables and the cold, wet stones worked their way into Sarah's shoes. O'Rafferty took his raincoat off and put it round her shoulders. An interminable row of stables containing single horses stretched out before them.

'Here's Britbuster for you,' said O'Rafferty. 'He's asleep. Let's go inside.'

'Is he really asleep, Uncle Seamus?' asked Sarah, trying to hide her terror of horses because they were bigger than she was.

'Sure, he's asleep. Can you not see that his eyes are closed? Come on in.'

He unbolted the door and ushered her in.

'Now, look, my pretty, little niece, it would be easier to go behind Britbuster.'

'But if you stand behind horses, they kick.'

'Not when they're asleep, they don't, silly. Come on. There's no need for all this fussing.'

He took her by the hand and led her to the back of the motionless horse. He had over-estimated the space available to them.

He lit a cigarette and gave one to Sarah. When they had finished smoking, O'Rafferty kissed her and unplaited her hair.

'I'm afraid we'll have to be standing,' he said abruptly.

Sarah suddenly had hysterical giggles.

'Would you be cutting your noise down. You'll wake Britbuster up.'

They only removed the clothing necessary for their purpose. She leapt up onto him. He was strong and able to hold her weight. His thick, black hair, combined with his loosened tie, set her blood on fire. Even in the uncomfortable position of standing up, he was an agile and vigorous lover. Her scream at the time of climax made Britbuster twitch in his sleep.

'I love you, Uncle Seamus, but the stable's not a suitable place for this.'

'No. Next time – that is tomorrow night – we'll have to use the attic after everyone's gone to bed.'

He gave her a fatherly kiss on the cheek. 'Goodnight, pretty, little Sarah.'

* * *

By the time she came down to breakfast the next morning, Sarah could tell instinctively that another monumental row had taken place. O'Rafferty had ordered Hattie and Biddy to leave the house again, because they had complained to Melissa about the affect that her drinking was having on the family. Melissa had complained to her husband that the two girls had been insulting her.

Biddy, who was livid with her mother because of the behaviour she exhibited when she was drunk, advanced towards Sarah as she came into the dining room.

'My mother *was* drunk last night, wasn't she, Sarah?' she demanded furiously.

Sarah was in a complicated enough situation already and was unwilling to take sides between a dipsomaniac woman and her children.

'Well, Sarah, wasn't she?'

'Y ... yes, Biddy!' Sarah eventually managed to splutter.

'And do you know where my mother is now?'

'No, Biddy!'

'I can tell you where she is. She's in bed, swigging away at the gin at nine-thirty in the morning.'

'Indeed?' said Sarah, who was obsessed by her affair with her uncle and on the point of tears of remorse through having abused her hostess's hospitality. She felt so confused that she was on the verge of confessing to Biddy, who had a sense of humour and would have taken it as a joke, enabling the act of laughter to assuage her guilt.

'Indeed? Indeed? Can you not say more than that? Do you know what she did to me this morning? When my bank statement came in, she snatched it from my hand, before I had a chance to open it and noticed that I had an overdraft of seventy pounds. She said she'd be cancelling my meagre allowance for what it's worth.'

'That's not a very nice thing to do. But where the drinking is concerned, if your mother's drunk, she's drunk. That's all there is to it. Besides, I haven't treated her too well myself.'

Biddy fixed her cousin with a fascinated stare.

'What did you do to her, Sarah?'

Sarah liked Biddy and decided to show off.

'Oh, I've been flirting with that beautiful father of yours a bit. I've been winking at him across the table. That sort of thing. God, he's attractive!'

Biddy gave her the audience she craved and began to giggle and Sarah laughed with her. She was mildly relieved to have got half the truth off her chest. It was as if she had bronchitis and had only hoiked up some of the phlegm, leaving the rest to form itself into a hard, unmovable lump.

Biddy continued to laugh.

'In what way have you been flirting with my father?'

'Oh, just catching his eye all the time. Raising my skirt a bit so that he can see my legs. Telling him saucy jokes.'

'Anything else?'

Sarah deliberately avoided looking her cousin in the eye.

'Oh, no, no!'

'My mother's drinking is totally out of control, Sarah. It's going to destroy the lot of us, including my father. The whole thing hurts him so much that he turns a blind eye to it, and when we try to talk to him about it, all he does is shout at us.'

Without warning, Sarah became acutely disturbed. She had no idea how to handle the situation.

'Damned, difficult problem!' she muttered.

O'Rafferty stormed into the room. It was a Sunday and he hadn't got up early to work on the farm. He advanced towards Biddy and grabbed her by the arm.

'I told you to get out of the house and the same goes for your sister! I want you both out now, whether you've packed your suitcases or not. I've also phoned every hotel in Dublin, saying that neither of you is to be admitted.'

As he spoke, the cook ran into the room, wringing her hands.

'There's an urgent call for you in the study, Mr O'Rafferty. It's from Belfast.'

O'Rafferty had a brother in Belfast called Jack who lived close to the Falls Road. Six months earlier, he had developed cancer but his doctors had told him that he had a fighting chance of recovery if he adhered to the necessary treatment, much of which was horrific. Hence, he had been a difficult and stubborn patient and had ignored his doctors.

O'Rafferty brushed past Biddy and rushed into the study.

'O'Rafferty here.'

'Sorry to trouble you, sir,' said a voice steeped in a Belfast accent.

'Yes, who's that?'

'My name is Kevin McTavish. I'm your brother Jack's next door neighbour.'

'Is Jack all right?' shouted O'Rafferty, who was close to his brother and only living sibling, their friendship bound tightly by their mutual, staunch republicanism.

'I'm afraid he's been took pretty poorly,' said McTavish.

'What, with cancer?'

'Aye. The doctor came last night and said that the disease was so advanced that he's not likely to last for another two days at most.'

'All right. I'll get on the first plane straight away. For

God's sake tell him that I'm coming. It may give him a little strength.'

Sarah was sitting in the garden, reading. Her uncle looked for her to say 'goodbye' but he couldn't find her. He packed a small, worn-out suitcase with S.O'R. engraved on it and left a note for Melissa. Then he eased himself behind the wheel of his green Ford Capri and hastened up the narrow lanes to Dublin until he reached the airport.

The airport was busy. The check-in queues were long and the oafish, young man in front of O'Rafferty monopolized the check-in clerk's time, talking animatedly about different brands of whisky. O'Rafferty heard a voice over the tannoy giving a final call to passengers bound for Belfast.

'Would you cut the crap, son,' rasped Seamus. 'My brother's dying.'

The man ignored him until O'Rafferty pushed him aside. A short scuffle took place until the man realized that O'Rafferty was much bigger than he was. He let the matter drop.

*   *   *

The sloping street in Belfast, where Jack O'Rafferty lived, was full of children and teenagers throwing stones which bounced off the transparent, riot shields of bored, British soldiers.

O'Rafferty walked down the street with his suitcase in one hand and a bouquet of flowers in the other. Some of the children throwing stones were as young as five.

'Pitch 'em up, lads! Pitch 'em up!' O'Rafferty called to the children.

A six-year-old boy, cursed with minimum intelligence, took his words so literally that he threw a stone at O'Rafferty, hitting him on the shoulder.

'No, no, you dumb nincompoop! Not at me. At the flaming soldiers!'

On the other side of the street, were walls covered with torn advertisements and anti-British graffiti in letters two feet high.

A group of middle-aged men had gathered on this side. Most of them wore baggy trousers. They were passing a bottle of beer to each other, singing a rabble-rousing rebel song with which O'Rafferty was familiar.

Armoured cars and tanks and guns
Came to take away our sons;
Every man must stand behind
The men behind the wire.

A drunk ran towards O'Rafferty and threw his arms round his neck. 'Welcome back to Belfast, Seamus. I'm afraid the commandant's very poorly.'

O'Rafferty grabbed the man by the arm and turned him away from the middle-aged men, facing the stone-throwing children and teenagers.

'How dare you use that word in a public place! What the hell are you trying to do – get us all jailed?'

'Sure, I'm sorry, Seamus. I won't do it again. It's just that it's such a grand surprise seeing you all of a sudden.'

'How's Jack, my brother?'

'He's still very ill. I'll be carrying your case for you and we'll get past these children and into his house.'

'Thanks,' said O'Rafferty.

The children and teenagers swiftly made a path for them like the division of the Red Sea. O'Rafferty patted a small child on the head. He knocked on the door of his brother's house and was let in by Kevin McTavish, whose off-white shirt sleeves had been rolled up to his elbows after giving Jack a blanket bath.

'You're a star, Kevin McTavish,' said O'Rafferty.

'' Tis nothing.' He ushered O'Rafferty into a damp room.

An Irish tricolour covered most of the wall and underneath it, was a simple, wooden crucifix. A huge statue of the Virgin Mary occupied the small bedside table and its size in relation to the table, looked ridiculous.

On another wall was a photograph of Jack and his brother in their late teens with bags slung over their shoulders as they took part in a republican patrol. Jack had his brother's dark hair and grey eyes but was not as tall as he.

The narrow bed in which the sick man lay, was covered with two threadbare blankets and a pile of copies of the *Irish Republican News*.

O'Rafferty rushed towards Jack and cradled his head in his arms while his brother struggled to suck air into his tumour-ridden lungs.

'Why the hell didn't you write?' asked O'Rafferty. 'At least I could have arranged to put you somewhere dry and warm. Apart from that, I didn't know the *Irish Republican News* was on sale in the north. 'Tis not a bad thing to be covering yourself up with.'

Jack started laughing. The more he laughed, the more his tightened airways became constricted.

'For God's sake, do something, Kevin!' shouted O'Rafferty to McTavish. 'His breathing's gone wrong. Go and call an ambulance.'

McTavish rushed outside since Jack wasn't on the telephone. Jack continued to smile and the two brothers embraced each other. Jack suddenly made a horrible, gurgling noise as blood spurted from his mouth. His eyes took on the glazed stare of death. O'Rafferty crossed himself and closed them. Then he lay on top of his brother's lifeless body and wept.

After some time, O'Rafferty left the house. One of the children in the street, aware of his predicament, pressed a rose into his hand.

'This is to give you hope,' said the child, a rough-looking eight-year-old boy, wearing blue jeans and a T-shirt with the word 'teamwork' painted on it.

O'Rafferty ruffled the boy's hair and muttered, 'Thank you, son.' The boy ran off and picked up a stone which he threw at a British soldier.

O'Rafferty stayed in Belfast for the funeral. Jack was buried with the Sinn Féin flag draped over his coffin. A long row of mourners, wearing black berets, dark glasses and leather jackets over black, polo-necked sweaters, thronged behind Jack O'Rafferty's coffin. A volley of shots, preceded by ritualistic shouts in Gaelic, was fired over his grave.

O'Rafferty helped to carry the feather-light coffin of the emaciated man and wept throughout the ceremony. When it was over, a few uniformed mourners, who had just made V-signs at a British helicopter hovering in the sky, patted him on the shoulder.

O'Rafferty didn't feel like talking to anyone. He left the cemetery, got systematically drunk in a pub and boarded the next plane to Dublin. The thing that bothered him most of all and drove him to the pub, was a feeling of conflict. He felt guilty because he had not contributed arduously enough towards the republican cause which his circumstances prevented him from doing, due to his duty towards his sick wife. In his gloomy state, another black thought invaded his mind. The difference between the old-style IRA with its courageous and noble ideals, contrasting with the new IRA which bombed innocent civilians, hurt and disillusioned him. He drank more on the plane and had to be escorted to a car by Shamie who had come to meet him. (Shamie later returned to the airport to collect his father's Ford Capri.)

* * *

62

Sarah made friends with Eileen during Hattie's and Biddy's absence. The two rebel sisters stayed in a flat rented by one of Biddy's friends at Trinity College. O'Rafferty had still not returned from Belfast and Eileen took Sarah to a wild party in Dublin, where recreational drugs were distributed as freely as alcohol, nuts and crisps.

Eileen wore a purple, sequined, low-cut vest and tight, leather trousers and her mane of black hair fell over her suntanned shoulders. She was flirting with two rough, heavily sweating men who looked as if they had come straight from a building site. The three of them circulated a joint and inhaled deeply. Eileen passed it to Sarah.

'I've never had one of these before. Will it make me ill?'

'Don't be so wet!' said Eileen while her two companions studied Sarah in her silk, yellow trousers and matching shirt, partly covered by her leopard-skin shawl.

Sarah felt self-conscious. She took the joint from Eileen's hand and inhaled it as deeply into her lungs as she could. She took several puffs and suddenly had hysterical giggles.

Eileen inhaled the joint a second time and passed it to the two men. She lowered her shoulder strap and flicked her hair in their faces. They ran their fingers through it, laughing.

'By the way, Sarah, I know all about you and my father. I know what happened that time he took you to see Britbuster,' said Eileen.

'How?' asked Sarah.

Eileen repeated her gesture of rolling back her head and shaking her hair.

'Never mind how I know. I also know about that evening when you got drunk and he kissed you in the study.'

Sarah suddenly caught Eileen's eye. Her liquid, grey eyes were identical to those of her father and equally as probing. Had she not been befuddled with hashish which increased her giggles, she would have blushed. Instead, she said, 'Does anyone else know? Your mother, for instance? I wouldn't want her to know.'

'It's all right. She doesn't know, so you can sleep peacefully in your bed tonight. No one knows but me and I won't tell anyone. I think the whole thing's hilarious.'

The cousins rolled about on the floor, laughing.

'Do you mean even Hattie and Biddy don't know?'

'No, they don't know but Biddy knows you fancy my father because you told her so.'

Sarah was more interested in talking about Eileen's life.

'I notice your sisters spend a lot of time together but you don't seem to have much contact with them.'

'Well, they think I'm a bit wild. Also, I can always make my father laugh when he gets into a bait. My sisters get so emotionally worked up, they can't do that.'

'Are you fond of them?'

'Yes. When it comes to a row, there is always camaraderie between us. Also, when our men ring us up, one of us keeps guard outside the door and the other occupies my mother so that she can't listen in on the line.'

The two men, who had introduced themselves as Flan and Buddy, had finished the joint and were looking for less pedestrian excitement.

'You two girls, talking to each other all the time, are you sisters?'

'No, first cousins. My name's Eileen O'Rafferty and this is Sarah Lloyd. She's English.'

'I know. I can tell by her accent,' said Buddy. 'Why don't we find something more interesting to take? All this stuff does is give us the bloody giggles.'

'Stay where you are,' Eileen said. 'I know what you're looking for.'

She went over to a corner of the room where a fifteen-year-old girl was lying on the floor, wearing a cotton dress rolled up over her naked breasts. Her eyes were rolled back and only the whites were showing. A hippy knelt over her, holding her hand, as she shouted that plants were growing out of her stomach covered by her own skin.

'It's OK. It's not real. You'll come down soon,' the hippy ventured in a frail tone.

Eileen went up to the hippy who was selling the tiny, white pills.

'How much are they each?'

'Ten pounds.'

'I'll have four, please.'

'Forty pounds,' said the hippy.

Eileen called across the room to Sarah and told her to come over.

'Have you got forty pounds? If you have, we'll all be able to have a go.'

Sarah turned away from the hippy and pulled out a wad of English banknotes. She gave forty pounds to Eileen who paid for the four pills. The girls went back to Flan and Buddy, both of whom swallowed the pills straight away, but the cousins wanted to wait a while and continued their talk.

'Have you found out about what's happening at home?' asked Eileen suddenly.

'My home or yours?'

'Mine, you big dope.'

'I know about your mother and her drinking, if that's what you mean.'

'It's much worse than you think. She was such a nice, kind person once and I like to think it's the drink that's speaking and not her sometimes. The drink has possessed her. Maybe it's not entirely her fault but it's made her cantankerous and destructive. The worst of it is that she's made out a Will, leaving her inheritance from her father

65

to Paddy and Shamie alone, her favourites. Hattie, Biddy, Sean and I have all been cut off without a penny.'

'What about your father? Surely, he can't allow this?'

'It's not that simple. In the first place, it's not his money. Also, he is so desperately in love with my mother that he is blind to her faults. He worships the ground she walks on.'

Sarah thought for a while.

'I don't understand. Your mother seems so nice. Why would she want to do something like that to her children? Not only that, to deliberately turn them against each other. Will Shamie and Paddy not distribute the money fairly after your mother dies?'

'They've both said they won't. We've been on to them.'

'Of course, they'd say they won't now. If they started showing loyalty towards the others, your mother would cut them out too. They're bound to relent after her lifetime. How did all this animosity start, anyway?' said Sarah.

The subject disturbed Eileen. She looked round the room to size up the men. When she found no one who attracted her more than Flan and Buddy, she turned to her cousin.

'After Paddy, the youngest of us, was born, my mother went into a state of nihilistic apathy which started her on the drink. Even though that was eight years ago, she still hasn't overcome either the melancholia or the alcoholism with which she tries to drown it.'

'Her suffering must be awful. Hasn't she consulted a doctor?'

'She can't stand doctors,' said Eileen, 'and you're right to say that her suffering must be awful. Even so, that doesn't justify her making others suffer as well. It's true I don't hate her as much as Hattie and Biddy do. Perhaps they had to put up with more from her in their teens than I did. I try to convince myself that there is more to life than money.'

'How can you think like that?' retorted Sarah. 'It's idiotic to say money's not important, and hypocritical too. Without money, what can you do? Where can you go?'

'All I care about is being free. When I pass my A levels, I want to travel all over Europe with an accordion and a group of singers. I don't particularly want to live in style. I want to lead a gypsy's life.'

On her mother's side, Sarah claimed to have gypsy ancestry. Her mother's sister, Miranda, an eccentric and a brilliant writer, was proud of her gypsy blood and encamped with gypsies while she was waiting for her books to be published. Sometimes she would join travelling circuses, another of her passions. She had a good sense of balance and rode on rearing elephants and stood up on horses. Miranda had died of a neglected illness during the Second World War so Sarah had never met her. Often, she would ask her mother what Miranda was like, to which she would get the unvaried reply: 'Oh, she was a very queer lady.'

Sarah was fascinated by Miranda and admired her guts and disregard of the importance of money, a characteristic that she envied. Her admiration for Eileen's ambitions increased, because she felt that she lacked her cousin's courage.

'I've always tried to convince myself that there is more to life than money,' Eileen repeated, adding, 'I try to be nice to my mother because I pity her. Somehow, I wonder whether she is really responsible for seeming wicked because fifty per cent of her is mad. Perhaps alcoholics suffer even more than their families.'

Sarah wondered how much of Eileen's story was true. She certainly felt less guilty about her relations with O'Rafferty. She was beginning to feel bored.

67

'Come on, Eileen, give me a pill.'

Eileen put a little, white, hallucinatory pill on her tongue and gave one to Sarah. The two girls lay on the floor looking at the ceiling, while the band ironically played a catchy pop song, the chorus of which was, *'Money, money, money in a rich man's world'*.

Ten minutes passed. Eileen was the first to break the silence.

'Look at the ceiling,' she said, pointing at the dingy, brown ceiling with most of its paint peeling off. She was staring at the bits of paint which were peeling off in curly shapes.

'This is like floating in the sky, looking at the sea. The curly bits are like silver, white horses mixed with different browns. All the colours are a mixture of rich blue, pink and gold.

Her drugged eyes wandered to a broad crack in the ceiling. 'There's a river flowing to the sea. It's so clear, I can see the safety pins and peas at the bottom of the river.'

Eileen had no idea what was happening to Sarah who found thick, wild moss growing on her arms. She tried to peel it off with her nails but it felt like granite. The physical pain she was inflicting on herself was unbearable. The moss seemed to be eating into her flesh.

She staggered over to the table that the food and drinks were on, and found a serrated-edged bread knife. She felt herself cutting into the moss with the ease of a surgeon until Flan and Buddy rushed over to her and forced the knife from her hand. They had taken the hallucinatory drug so frequently that the effect it had on them was minimal. They merely felt as if they had had too much to drink.

Buddy rushed over to Eileen and tried to shake her to her senses.

'For Christ's sake, wake up! We need you to help us to take your cousin upstairs. She's been cutting the skin off her arms.'

Eileen could see the horrifying state that Sarah's arms were in but her head was so light she couldn't take it in.

The men laid Sarah down on an unmade bed. Eileen knelt beside her and held her hand.

'I don't think this is as serious as it looks,' she said feebly.

'We'll have to take her to hospital,' said Buddy.

They helped Sarah out of the house, so as not to implicate the host, and went to a phone booth. Flan called for an ambulance, while Eileen sat on the pavement with her arms round Sarah who was screaming.

'Rather bad burns on arms,' said Buddy down the line. 'Someone fell into a brazier.'

'For God's sake shut your eyes,' said Eileen in a whisper, 'or you'll land us all in it.'

Sarah was taken to Accident and Emergency on a stretcher, and her companions were told to sit in the waiting area, after being ticked off for making too much noise.

A young Pakistani doctor came into Sarah's cubicle. A nurse stated, if superfluously, that her arms had been damaged and Eileen was called in to answer questions as Sarah couldn't speak coherently.

'Are you her friend?' asked the doctor.

'Yes. We're first cousins.'

'How did her arms get into that state?' asked the nurse.

'She and I were walking down the street, looking for a restaurant. An IRA man overheard her English accent and pushed her into a chestnut seller's brazier. It's more than likely he resented her for wearing leopard skin,' added Eileen spontaneously, if not very intelligently.

'Do IRA men normally push people into braziers because they're wearing leopard skin?' asked the Pakistani.

69

Eileen lost her temper. 'For Christ's sake, that was a bloody stupid question! The IRA aren't products of one identical clone. Besides, my cousin would hate having to stay overnight in hospital. Once she's bandaged up, I'm taking her home.'

'I still think she should see the duty psychiatrist.'

'She has a morbid fear of psychiatrists. Once her arms are bandaged up, I'll be taking her home and you can't stop me!'

Sarah's arms were washed and bandaged by the nurse who left the cousins alone with the doctor. Sarah was coming round and her eyes came into focus.

'Would you mind leaving us alone for a moment?' Eileen said.

The doctor left the cubicle and stood outside.

'It was my fault. I shouldn't have given in to you when you asked for it,' said Eileen.

'No, it wasn't. I knew it was LSD and I knew exactly what I was doing. It's too late to go home. I want to go to a hotel. I've got plenty of credit so I'll pay.'

'Are you sure?'

'Yes, quite sure. I just don't want any involvement with the Dublin police.'

'Oh, there's no risk of that,' said Eileen. 'You must have had a terrible time. Why did you take all the skin off your arms?'

'Because they were covered in moss.'

'Moths?' asked the Pakistani doctor who had been listening outside.

'I thought I asked you to leave us alone,' said Eileen irritably. 'Yes, she has an allergy to moths. They make her skin itch and that's why she's scratched the skin off her arms.'

Before the doctor could mention the brazier about which Eileen had spoken earlier, Eileen helped her cousin

70

out of bed and dragged her out of the hospital. The nurse was talking to the receptionist who warned her that they had escaped, but the nurse was slow-witted because of exhaustion and felt unable to catch up with them.

The cousins hailed a taxi and Eileen asked the driver to take them to a hotel. He skidded dangerously through the rain-soaked, Dublin streets. He, too, was worn out and wanted to go home.

'What are we going to say to your father?' asked Sarah.

'There'll be no problem there. He's not coming back from Belfast until the day after tomorrow. Your arms may have healed a bit by then. I'll say you have an allergy to a certain kind of washing powder and that it didn't affect your hands because you were wearing rubber gloves.'

* * *

O'Rafferty looked a broken man on his return from Belfast. He went straight to Britbuster's stable, caressed his favourite horse and wept.

Eileen and Sarah were playing chess in the living room. They had already played two games and Sarah, who was a poor player, cheated throughout, whenever her cousin looked the other way.

'Sarah, you wicked Brit, you've been cheating. I saw you move your knight on to a square so that it could take my bishop and on top of that, you said you hadn't made your move yet. You cheat!'

O'Rafferty's absence had taken its toll on Sarah and she got angry.

'How dare you accuse me of cheating? I wasn't cheating! I was just rearranging some of my men.'

O'Rafferty suddenly entered the room, wearing the clothes he had left in, his gait uncharacteristically slow, his face pale and haggard and his head lowered. His eyes were red from drinking and weeping.

71

Eileen sprang to her feet, ran to her father and kissed him.

'I'm so sorry about poor Uncle Jack, Da.'

As they remained in an embrace, a wave of jealousy surged through Sarah. She took Eileen's queen off the board and checked her unprotected king with her castle. Then she got up, her bandaged arms hidden by an obscenely tight sweater. She took the gift-wrapped bottle of Cointreau she had bought over to O'Rafferty, who released his hold on Eileen and grabbed hold of the gift like a child.

'Sarah, my pretty, little niece! It was the hope that you'd still be here that's kept me alive over the last few days. Give your uncle a kiss.'

Because Eileen was in the room, the embrace was no more than that between a father and daughter.

'Playing chess, eh?' said O'Rafferty, trying to take his mind off his misery. 'Don't let me interrupt your game.'

Eileen noticed the absence of her queen and her unprotected king threatened by Sarah's castle. She flew into a violent rage, flaunting her father's genes.

'Where's my queen? You've taken it off the board, you cheating Brit!

'Stop accusing me of cheating,' said Sarah, 'and added to that, it's checkmate.'

Eileen brushed the board and the pieces off the table.

'I'm not playing with you again, Sarah. You're a filthy cheat and I don't play games with cheats.'

Because the row between the girls was disconnected with the sensitive subject of his wife's drinking habits, O'Rafferty found it comical that someone should get away with cheating at chess. He laughed hysterically as if laughter were a form of vomit ejecting his grief.

'Come on, you silly pair. Let's go to my study and drink Sarah's bottle of Cointreau.'

The liquor was more intoxicating than either of the cousins had experienced before. They soon forgot their quarrel and wept with O'Rafferty.

Late that night, the uncle and niece climbed up to the attic and had violent, noisy, upstanding sex to commemorate their love, which had become so intense that it no longer caused them joy but pain.

Melissa happened to be staggering along the corridor beneath the attic on her way downstairs to get another bottle of gin. She heard noises from above but was too drunk to understand what was going on.

She woke her husband at nine o'clock the next day which was a Sunday.

'I heard a lot of noise in the attic last night. I looked for you but you weren't around. Have we got rats?'

'Racks?' asked O'Rafferty, stalling his words before deciding how to flirt with danger.

'Rats, I said.'

'Rats? No, no, I went up there to get to my old chest. I was looking for letters from Jack. I couldn't find the key so I had to force it open with a knife.'

Melissa took a swig of gin regardless of the early hour. She appeared satisfied with O'Rafferty's explanation. He turned over and held her.

'What the hell did you think I was doing up there? Playing bowls?'

O'Rafferty had discussed his affair with his niece with his priest but, because Melissa had deceived him occasionally in the past, he felt no guilt. He loved his wife just as dearly as he loved his niece and, although he felt sorry for Melissa because she had aged in comparison with her rival, he was spiritually comfortable about his behaviour.

'I thought I heard a woman's voice in the attic,' said Melissa. 'I feel sure she was screaming.'

O'Rafferty turned away from his wife to hide the blush that had come to his cheeks.

'Screaming? What are you talking about? There wasn't a woman screaming up there as far as I know and I'm sure I would have heard her if there was. I think you'd had too much to drink. Jaysus, I wish you'd cut it down. Do you think I enjoy beating the children when they tell you to do the same thing?'

'Oh, Seamus, they're all so foul to me!'

'Please, Melissa, don't talk about that now. For Christ's sake, I've just lost my brother. Don't you know that?'

Melissa didn't reply. She had drifted off into a drunken sleep.

* * *

Sarah came down to breakfast at nine-thirty the next morning and found her uncle drinking one cup of coffee after the other, chain smoking.

'Hullo, little one. How would you like to come out with Eileen and me in my old horse and cart?'

The Spartan cart was pulled by a rust-coloured pony called Dixie which had been in the O'Rafferty family for over five years. The trio sat on hard, uncomfortable seats. O'Rafferty was beginning to feel a little better as he took the reins.

'Come on, my lasses, let's have a song.'

'All right,' said Eileen, 'what about *Some Say the Devil, is Dead*?'

'Nice song,' said O'Rafferty who broke into song between inhaling his cheroot.

Some say the Devil is dead,
The Devil is dead, the Devil is dead;
Some say the Devil is dead
And buried in Kilarney.

O'Rafferty slowed down to speak to a man waving to him.

'The very top of the morning to you, Mr O'Rafferty! I see you've still got your old mare. How's she doin'?'

'Ticking over nicely, thanks, Mr McMahon.'

O'Rafferty waved goodbye to his friend and shook the reins.

'Now, let's hear you sing along with me, girls, like you sang outside that Brigadier's bedroom when you were little. Come on. I can't be doing with shyness. Sing up.'

The girls obeyed.

I would say he rose again,
He rose again, he rose again;
I would say he rose again
And joined the British Army.

*   *   *

The next few days passed without dramatic, domestic incidents. Melissa was admitted to hospital for three days as a non-urgent case to have tests performed on her liver. O'Rafferty was subdued and gloomy and his mood only lifted on occasions when he was entertained by his pretty, cheerful and vivacious niece.

It was a Monday morning. O'Rafferty had not gone out to the farm before daybreak, as was his habit on weekdays, when he took Paddy with him to milk the cows.

When Sarah had had her breakfast, she assumed that her uncle was out on the farm. She had lost an earring and went to his study where they had had violent and savage sex on the floor the night before. Sarah found that the door was locked.

'Is there anyone in there? Uncle Seamus, is that you?'

When no answer came, she assumed that her uncle had hidden something in his study and had taken the key with him. She suddenly felt depressed and sought the company of Eileen, who was still asleep. She forced herself to shake off her black mood and sat by the log fire in the living room, reading a biography of Rachmaninov. She favoured biographies more than novels but she found this book amazingly boring. Indeed, it told her little about the composer, and too much about his attitude towards the Russian countryside.

She looked in the mirror over the mantelpiece and wished that she could float through it into eternity like Alice. It was twelve noon. She went to the drinks tray and poured herself a large gin and tonic.

Sarah had no idea that her uncle was sitting behind the locked door of his study, gloomily brooding and chain-smoking. His mood had deteriorated to despair. He had lost his brother. He feared that Melissa's liver function assays would show terminal cirrhosis and lastly, he was thinking in a painfully obsessive manner about his role in the operations of the IRA.

He remembered the black thoughts which had plagued him on his way home from Belfast after his brother's funeral. The manner in which the IRA's face had changed from the old days tortured O'Rafferty, who had been involved in the loss of civilian lives in Ireland and across the water.

As he grew bored with smoking cigarettes, he took some tobacco from his drawer to fill his pipe with, and tried to reason with himself, in an effort to end the mental conflict which so depressed him.

He told himself that Protestants in Ulster had a tendency to treat Catholics like lackeys, and to discriminate against them at job interviews, rendering seventy per cent of them unemployed. He took note of the fact that Protestant settlers had abused Irish natives for hundreds of years and burnt down their cottages when their rents were in arrears.

As these and other bitter thoughts passed through his mind, a feeling of viciousness came over him. 'What the hell was wrong with an eye for an eye and a tooth for a tooth?' he asked himself. In view of what had happened to his fellow Catholic countrymen, both historically and currently, how could the odd civilian casualty, which he liked to call 'civvie cazh', possibly be avoided? After all, he reasoned, innocent children in German cities were bombed by the Allies during the Second World War.

He leant forward and supported his head with his hands as another conflicting thought hit him. Surely, the Germans had behaved far worse than the British. At least the British had never rounded up Irish rebels and thrown them into gas chambers.

But such comparisons are irrelevant, he told himself.

'Yes. I must help my comrades get the British out of the north,' he muttered out loud. 'And if that means a highly unfortunate succession of bombing campaigns on the British mainland, with the odd civvie cazh chucked in, then it must still be done.'

He took the rolled up republican flag from his drawer and fondled it as if it were a woman's petticoat. He banged on his desk, relieved to have come to terms with this particular conflict. He clambered on to the desk, manically waving the flag in the air.

'*Erin go bragh!*'* he shouted.

He jumped to the floor and poured himself a whisky and soda. Then he sat in his armchair by the window and continued to smoke his pipe.

His thoughts turned to Sarah. Of course, no one in his family knew of his political activities, except Melissa, to whom he had confessed after a few whiskies, but who wasn't interested in the first place. He had fallen hopelessly

* Ireland forever!

in love with Sarah whom he knew had hailed from a prosperous, British family. He felt he trusted her, however, due to her dog-like devotion and loyalty towards him. Yes, he *would* tell her and she *would* be tutored by him and follow him when called upon to do so.

Sarah appeared to have no strong feelings of patriotism towards her own country. He regarded her as an intensely vain, jolly child – a child so besotted with him that there was an overwhelming chance that he could win her loyalty towards his cause by gentle manipulation. He knew also that intrigue and the need to keep secrets delighted her.

He felt refreshed and relieved by the myriad of thoughts that had flashed through his mind and the conclusions that he had reached. He put his pipe back in the drawer and strode through the house to find his fresh, new love, who was sitting reading.

O'Rafferty sat on the sofa by her side and kissed her on the cheek.

'Hullo, my little angel.'

'Hullo, Uncle Seamus.'

O'Rafferty put his arm round her waist. 'I love the way you keep calling me "Uncle Seamus". It is the very innocence that is the aphrodisiac.'

'What makes you think I'm so innocent?'

O'Rafferty avoided the question.

'What's that book you've got there, Sare?'

No one had ever called her 'Sare' before. She liked the way her uncle had abbreviated her name.

'It's an amazingly boring biography of Rachmaninov. It tells you nothing about the composer's personality at all.'

'Rachmaninov? He's one of my favourite composers. He wrote the famous second piano concerto in C minor, didn't he?'

Sarah had known all along that her rough-spoken uncle

was cultured. His knowledge of the concerto fuelled her love for him.

'I can play it if you want,' said O'Rafferty as he walked over to the piano, 'but only the first few bars.'

He could indeed only play the first few bars but he played beautifully. He returned to Sarah's side and sat down.

'It's a pity you brought a book which has disappointed you,' he said, attempting to sound casual. 'I have a few books about Irish history upstairs. They're nicely written. Would you like to try one?'

'Yes, I think I would.'

'Do you know anything about Irish history?'

Sarah put her cigarette out and ran her hands through her hair, which she was wearing loose. She was relieved not to have to disgrace herself by pleading ignorance.

'I know the Anglo-Irish problem started in 1172 during the reign of King Henry II of England. He sent his armies to Ireland when the country was split into kingdoms, headed by chieftains permanently at war with each other. King Henry intervened to negotiate a peace settlement.

'Since his reign, English monarchs tried their hands at sorting out Irish affairs, gradually gaining more and more monopoly of the country. The Earl of Essex in Elizabeth's reign may be a folk hero in English history but he instituted a campaign to persecute the Irish, and since Elizabeth's reign and the Reformation, which heralded a line of Protestant kings, things got very much worse. Protestant settlers, in particular, set up home in Ireland and gave a lot of flak to Irish Catholics, whose families had lived there for hundreds of years.'

O'Rafferty interrupted her. 'Jaysus, Sarah, how do you know all this? Irish history isn't taught in English schools.'

'It was you who taught me, Uncle Seamus, when I was little. It was about the same time that you paid me half a crown to sing Irish rebel songs outside that Brigadier's bedroom. You must remember. I asked you once what an Irish rebel song was and, one day, you took me out for a walk and gave me an Irish history lesson.'

O'Rafferty was astounded. 'What a rare memory you have, my golden, little lassie!' He began to caress her gently and wind her hair round his hand. 'Your hair's grown since you came to stay. It's so lovely. Go on now, tell me what else you know about this country's history.'

'Well, I don't know that much but I'll tell you what little I do know. The situation deteriorated when William of Orange came to the throne in 1689. The north of Ireland was colonized by Protestant settlers, some from England, some from Holland. Antagonism against Catholics was severe. They lost the Battle of the Boyne when the Protestant armies besieged Londonderry, which had been surrounded by Catholics. The Protestants liberated their fellow Protestants held in captivity there.

'Also, and particularly in the eighteenth and nineteenth centuries, the plight of Irish Catholics got worse. Their thatched cottages were burnt down by English landlords, who had settled in Ireland, when the cottage dwellers were unable to pay their rents which kept going up.

'After the Easter Rebellion of 1916, under the leadership of Sir Roger Casement, who was executed, independence was granted to the southern Irish counties but Protestant-governed Ulster remained, and still does, a British colony.'

'Come on, Sare, let's go to my study and have a drink. Your memory is overwhelming.'

Sarah gave a coy, girlish giggle. 'I'm afraid I only have vague ideas about Irish history. I wish I knew more and I'd like to see your books about it, provided they're not as boring as the book I'm reading at the moment.'

80

O'Rafferty suddenly looked offended.

'What is it, Uncle Seamus? Did I say something wrong?'

Tears came into O'Rafferty's eyes. 'It was my brother, Jack, who wrote them books. He was a professional historian,' he said hoarsely.

Sarah got up and walked two paces backwards. 'Oh, Uncle Seamus, I'm so sorry. How awful! I should have known.'

'It's all right,' said O'Rafferty. He grabbed his niece by the hand. 'Come on, let's go to my study and you can help yourself to some whisky.'

'May I ask you a question, Uncle Seamus?' she asked as they entered the study.

'Of course you can, lassie.'

'I thought of using yours and Aunt Melissa's bedroom, seeing she's not here, but that would really be a sin, I think.'

'Yes, I wouldn't be prepared to do that. Come on, drink up your whisky like a good girl.'

Sarah had not realized what a stupendous lover her uncle was. His imaginative foreplay, followed by his gentle entry and the way in which he became rougher and rougher as he reached a climax, was a drug to which she was addicted and would never again be able to do without. His method lacked even the remotest inhibition and because his performance was prolonged for at least twenty minutes, she was able to ejaculate repeatedly and copiously, while he rubbed her clitoris and breasts throughout.

'Don't scream now, lassie,' muttered O'Rafferty. 'I'm not sure who's in the house at the moment.'

They rolled over and she sat astride him. She wanted to scream but he put his hand over her mouth. Once the act had terminated, the lovers rolled over and over on the floor, clutching at pieces of furniture.

'Sure, you're a rare, wee lover, my little lassie!' said

O'Rafferty once he had recovered his breath. He sat in his armchair by the window. 'Come and sit on my knee. We have to talk.'

Sarah obeyed, fearing that her uncle meant to terminate the affair.

'I've got three things to tell you and you might find them unpleasant.'

'Yes?' Sarah whitened.

'Melissa's liver function tests were phoned through to me by her consultant at the clinic in Dublin this morning. She's got what is known as pre-cirrhosis which means that if she doesn't stop drinking altogether, she will get proper cirrhosis which will kill her.'

'I'm so sorry, Uncle Seamus.'

'It will mean that what's going on between you and me will no longer continue in this house, once she comes home. It's too risky. We'll have to go to a hotel somewhere.'

'I don't mind that.'

'The second thing is poor Britbuster has got a nasty eye infection. It's so bad that he might go completely blind and lose his usefulness. Oh, Sarah, I adore that horse. It would break my heart if he lost his sight.'

'But he may not. You shouldn't be so pessimistic.'

'The vet's due to ring me in half an hour, to say when he'll be coming this evening.'

'This vet, is he any good?'

'I believe he is. He's cured all my animals when they've been ill in the past.'

Sarah embraced her uncle.

'Then of course, it's going to be all right. He may just need a course of antibiotic injections.'

Sarah and O'Rafferty sat in the armchair for two hours without speaking. For part of the time they slept. The phone rang at six-thirty. O'Rafferty picked up the receiver hurriedly and barked down it, subconsciously thinking that if bad news were to be broken, his bark would somehow chase it away.

'O'Rafferty!' he shouted.

'Good evening to you, sir. This is Cassidy.'

'When are you coming, Mr Cassidy?'

'I'm getting into my car now. I'll be there in half an hour. It's the horse's eyes, you say?'

'Yes,' gasped O'Rafferty. 'I'm terrified he'll lose his sight.'

'Oh, I'm sure that can be avoided, sir. Just keep calm. I'll be with you soon.'

O'Rafferty replaced the receiver, feeling better.

'You will be with me when Mr Cassidy comes, won't you, Sarah?'

'Don't worry. I'll be with you for as long as you need me, and I hope I can say the same for you.'

He sat down and she mounted his knee once more.

'Uncle Seamus?'

'Yes.'

'You said you were going to tell me three unpleasant things. You've told me two. What's the third?'

'I can't tell you the third thing now. I don't think I could get it out until I know that Britbuster will be all right.'

'But you're making me so nervous. Just tell me this: Is it anything to do with anyone in the family?'

'No.'

'Is it anything to do with our relationship?'

'No.'

'Is it any bad news about someone in my family?'

'Oh, Jaysus, no! It's something entirely different. It's no tragedy but it's going to jolt you a little. I'll tell you once I know that Britbuster's going to be all right, but not before.'

Mr Cassidy was one of Dublin's most prestigious vets.

83

He looked considerably younger than he did when Edward Biddle had consulted him about his dog. Cassidy had a gentle disposition and his love for whisky and beer had caused his face to be a permanent shade of pink.

He drove his old, white car up O'Rafferty's drive. He got out and walked towards the front door and rang the bell. O'Rafferty opened the door, his black hair ruffled and his shirt and zip undone. He was still exhausted from his carnal energy expenditure.

'Thanks so much for coming so quickly, Mr Cassidy.'

Cassidy came straight to the point. 'Where's your horse, Mr O'Rafferty?'

O'Rafferty escorted Cassidy and Sarah to the stable where they found Britbuster lying down in the straw. His eyes had got worse. Their whites had turned red, and a white, purulent fluid leaked from them and ran down his face.

The pathetic spectacle broke O'Rafferty's heart. He embraced the sick animal and wept out loud.

Sarah came in and held his hand, but was jealous of the horse, now commanding more of her uncle's attention than she was. 'It's going to be all right, Uncle Seamus, I know it is,' she said feebly.

O'Rafferty ignored her.

'What's wrong with my horse, Mr Cassidy?'

'Just let me get by and I'll take a look.' The vet opened his bag.

He examined Britbuster's eyes with a variety of instruments as the horse winced and neighed with pain.

'It's best you come in, sir,' said Cassidy. 'You'll have to hold him while I give him a couple of shots.'

O'Rafferty went in and put his arms round the horse's neck to hold him steady.

'What the blazes is wrong with him, Mr Cassidy?'

'Nothing as serious as it looks. Of that I am sure.

He has an eye infection and inflamed retinas to prevent him seeing. I can clear this up in a week with anti-biotics. But he does need a strong painkiller which I'll be injecting him with now, together with a syringe full of Erythromycin.'

'What the hell's Erythromycin?' asked O'Rafferty.

'A broad spectrum antibiotic. It can be used on humans as well as animals.'

O'Rafferty held the horse steady while Cassidy gave him two injections in the backside, one a painkiller, the other an antibiotic. Sarah watched, while her jealousy of her uncle's love for the horse increased.

When Cassidy had finished and the painkiller had taken effect, he eased the horse to his feet and put his instruments back in his bag.

'I'll need to come back tomorrow, Mr O'Rafferty, and once a day for a week. Would the same time suit you?'

'Yes. That'll be fine. What's the prognosis? Is my horse going to recover his sight?'

Cassidy removed his cap and scratched his head. 'Certainly, he will. Some other horses in this area have had the same infection but I've no idea what the cause of it is. It will comfort you to know that they're all better now.'

O'Rafferty shook the vet's hand. 'Thank you, so much, Mr Cassidy. See you tomorrow, then.'

'Yes, Mr O'Rafferty, I'll be there.'

Cassidy got into his car and reversed down the long drive, finding nowhere appropriate to turn round. O'Rafferty put his arm on Sarah's shoulder.

'I'm so relieved. How about the barn, this time? I'm in the mood.'

Sarah's mood was petulant and fractionally less compliant with O'Rafferty's wishes this time.

'Tell me, Uncle Seamus,' she said, turning towards him,

'if Britbuster and I were floating out to sea on a raft and you only had the choice of saving one of us, which one would you save?'

O'Rafferty was taken aback. He wondered whether Sarah had developed hostile feelings towards him.

'Sure, that's a damned silly question! I'd save my little lassie, of course. A human is dearer than a horse, however superb the horse may be.'

Sarah threw her arms round her uncle's neck.

'Come on, let's go to the barn, Uncle Seamus!'

He picked her up and carried her into the barn, where he laid her down and pushed his hands under her tight, cashmere sweater, excited by the fact that she wasn't wearing a bra.

'For Christ's sake make it rough, you beautiful, big, Irish hulk!' she shouted.

O'Rafferty obliged. This time, their performance was more bestial than before. The lovers rolled over and over screaming.

'What the hell's all that noise? Jaysus, I can hear me Da. He'll murder me for taking you to the barn.'

This was the voice of O'Rafferty's handsomest son, Sean, aged sixteen. He was a jockey who rode his father's horses. He had picked up a prostitute in a Dublin street with the somewhat curious name of Bluebell.

'Put on your clothes and hurry up about it. Come on! We're getting out of here,' Sean said in a horse whisper.

Sean and Bluebell had lain down behind two bales of hay. Neither of them had made a sound for fear of being found by O'Rafferty's farm manager, who would have reported them to his boss had he seen them. The noise made by O'Rafferty himself on the other side of the bales seemed like an auditory hallucination.

'I'll give you a fiver for this,' whispered Sean. 'I don't think me Da knows we're here.'

'Who's he got with him?' asked Bluebell. 'Another loose woman from Dublin?'

'Keep your fockin' voice down! I suspect he's been with my cousin.'

Bluebell's immediate circumstances were too extraordinary for her simple, bird-witted mind to come to terms with.

'Then your father must be taking his own niece. That's incest, isn't it?'

'I don't know if he's with my cousin or not. Anyway, they're not blood relations, so stop asking daft questions.'

'Don't forget, you owe me a fiver for my services. May I have my money now so that I can get back to my beat?' said Bluebell.

'All right, all right!' Sean dragged a five-pound note from his inside pocket and gave it to her.

Sarah had been lying on the floor of the barn as contented and as satiated as a cat after drinking a saucer of cream.

'I think I can hear voices, Uncle Seamus, coming from over there.' She pointed towards the bales of hay.

O'Rafferty was as embarrassed as an adolescent boy who had wet the bed in someone else's house. 'Put on your clothes and go straight back to the house. I can't afford to have you seen,' he told Sarah.

She did as she was told. There was a heavy thunderstorm. She changed into dry clothes and sat in the living room, reading.

O'Rafferty's secretary, Mrs Cashin, a woman in a neat, grey suit and glasses, with her dark brown hair coiled on top of her head, knocked and came in.

'Miss Lloyd?'

'Yes?' Sarah's immediate reaction was fear of being notified of someone's death.

'The hospital called this afternoon to say that Mrs

O'Rafferty's discharging herself prematurely. She'll be back in time for dinner. Perhaps you could inform Mr O'Rafferty.'

'Why can't you inform him yourself?'

'Because I've no idea where he is.'

'Leave a message on his desk in his study, then. I don't know where he is either.'

'Can't you do so?'

Sarah was depressed by the fact that her love for her uncle was totally out of control. She couldn't stand this office-attired figure standing over her while she remained seated.

'I'm not Mr O'Rafferty's secretary,' she replied. 'I am his guest. You took the message so you must deliver it yourself.'

* * *

O'Rafferty dressed hurriedly and shambled like a drunk over to the bales of hay dividing him from his son.

'What the hell are you doing, Sean?'

'Oh, Da, this is my friend, Bluebell. She came to visit me this afternoon. We went for a walk and came here to shelter from the rain.'

'Bluebell who?' rasped O'Rafferty.

Sean didn't know the answer to that question.

'Bluebel – er – er.'

'Bluebell O'Farrell,' said the girl confidently. 'How do you do, sir?'

Bluebell was wearing a short, purple miniskirt and a matching, purple T-shirt with a caption showing the words, 'I'm yours' on it. O'Rafferty thought that the T-shirt was vulgar but he regarded her depraved-looking face and fishnet stockings with interest.

'I heard money changing hands, Sean,' he shouted.

'I know. I owed her a fiver because of a bet I lost on a horse.'

'What are you holding in your hand, Sean?'

'Nothing, Da.'

'Open your fist immediately!'

Sean lowered his head and trembled with fear of his father. He obeyed.

'A used contraceptive? A condom? By God, I won't tolerate your using one of those, you godless infidel. I bet you'll be excommunicated from the Catholic Church before you die, you foul, worthless, reprobate lout! You have caused me nothing but pain throughout your life, and your poor mother, too.'

By this time, Bluebell had run off. She was only fourteen and not old enough to cope with the wrath of a furious, middle-aged man.

'Sean, come over here!'

Sean was terrified and obeyed.

'That girl isn't a friend of yours. She's a prostitute. Do you take me for a fool?'

'No, Da,' the boy eventually managed to splutter.

O'Rafferty came so close to his son that they almost touched each other.

'You fornicated with that girl without even knowing her surname, didn't you?'

'Sure, I know, Da, but it slipped my memory when you came and startled me.'

O'Rafferty gave his son a clip on the ear.

'There's no need to hit me, Da.'

O'Rafferty picked up one of the bales of hay and threw it across the barn in an attempt to assuage his rage.

'You won't know what hitting is before I've finished with you in my study!'

Sean was given a sound thrashing in his father's study which ended when the older man's arm was exhausted. His father collapsed in one of the armchairs when his energy expenditure had burnt out his wrath.

'Oh, Sean, my boy, whatever are we going to do with you, eh?'

'I'm really sorry, Da.'

'So am I. Go on, help yourself to a drink.'

Sean's shaking hand filled a glass with some sherry. He walked slowly over to another chair and sat down opposite his father. The sherry gave him the courage to ask his father what he so desperately wanted to know.

'Da?'

'Yes, son.'

'I heard you making an awful lot of noise in the barn before you found me. What were you doing?'

O'Rafferty slowly put some tobacco into his pipe and lit it.

'I don't know why you ask. I was trying to shift a heavy piece of machinery which the farm manager had put in the barn to protect it from the storm.'

Sean drained his glass of sherry and leant forward in his chair.

'I heard a woman's voice, too, Da. It sounded like Sarah's.'

O'Rafferty couldn't find his words. He walked slowly to the window which he opened and then closed. He walked back to his chair.

'As you know, Britbuster's been ill with inflamed eyes. The vet, Mr Cassidy, called this afternoon to give him an antibiotic injection. He'll be coming to give him injections every afternoon for a week. Sarah wanted to come with me to see Britbuster and she was terribly upset on witnessing the pain he was in. She got a bit hysterical as, being English, she gets very sentimental about animals.

'When the storm started, I took her to the barn to keep her dry. She wasn't wearing a raincoat or anything. I saw a piece of machinery and she offered to help me shift it. It proved to be too heavy for her and she sprained

90

a muscle and started screaming. Anything else you want to know?'

Sean was silent for a while. He helped himself to another glass of sherry.

'Yes, there is something else I'd like to know, Da. Are you having an affair with Sarah?'

O'Rafferty leapt to his feet, went over to where his son was sitting and gave him a thunderous slap on the ear. 'How dare you be so disgustingly insolent! I've been in love with your dear mother since the day I met her. Nothing in the world would induce me to have another woman. Besides, young Sarah's little more than a child. She's my niece, for Christ's sake,' O'Rafferty said, adding, 'Incidentally, your hair needs cutting.'

'Jesus Christ wore his hair long, so why shouldn't I?' said the boy.

'Jaysus Chroist may have worn his hair long,' bellowed O'Rafferty, 'but Jaysus Chroist didn't happen to be roydin' any of my fockin' hosses!'

O'Rafferty left the study and went into the living room where Sarah sat reading.

'Hullo, Sare. I'm going to the garage. Come and follow me in ten minutes. I've got something to tell you.'

'Ah! The third thing you were going to tell me?'

'No, Sare, I can't tell you that yet. Just follow after me.'

When Sarah reached the garage, O'Rafferty closed the thick, iron gate behind him.

'Get into the Land Rover, lassie,' he commanded.

She got in and leaned against her uncle.

'What the hell's going on?' she asked.

O'Rafferty put his arm round her shoulders. 'I'm hopelessly in love with you, but we can't carry this on here in Ireland. It's too dangerous.'

'Why?'

'Because Melissa's coming home from hospital tonight

of her own volition. My secretary gave me this information when I got back to the house. As you know, Melissa's liver is in a pre-cirrhotic state and her doctors have forbidden her to have any alcohol at all. If she finds out about us, she will hit the bottle with such a vengeance that she will get terminal cirrhosis of the liver.'

Sarah felt jealous and let down. 'I don't understand. I've been here for weeks and she's never found out.'

'I thought I could take the risk then because I didn't know about her liver. Have your parents finished having your room in London redecorated yet?'

'Yes,' said Sarah, now in tears, 'but I don't want to go back.'

'You'll have to, lassie. You'll have to go back. I can't take the risk.'

'Who do you really love – her or me?' shouted Sarah, but her uncle was moved rather than angered by her sudden display of jealousy.

'Can't you see? I'm in love with you both but she is sick and you are healthy. Besides, certain affairs here have made it necessary for me to stay in London for a while. We could meet there in safety and until I go there, you can ring me every evening at six o'clock on my private line.'

Sarah felt more comfortable. At the beginning of the discussion, she had feared that O'Rafferty would be ending their affair.

'What are these so-called "certain affairs" that bring you to London?' she asked.

'That's where we come to the third thing I have to tell you, Sarah.'

'Can't you tell me now?'

A loud knock could suddenly be heard at the garage door.

'Seamus, dear, I'm back.'

O'Rafferty's heart skipped a beat.

'Lie down on the floor, Sarah,' he commanded. 'Don't come out for another fifteen minutes.' O'Rafferty forced the door open. He was shocked to see that his wife had lost a lot of weight and looked very frail. 'Come on into the house, old girl, or you'll get a cold. I'll order tea.'

'Seamus?' Melissa asked suddenly.

'What?'

'Why had you locked yourself in the garage?'

'I wasn't locked in. The door closed on me, that's all. Perhaps you tried to open it but found it too heavy. I just went in to see if my binoculars were in the Land Rover.'

'I thought I heard you talking in there.'

'I suppose you could call it talking. I was cursing because they weren't there, blast it!'

'Where's Sarah? I hope she hasn't gone home yet.'

'Sarah? Oh, yes, Sarah. Her mother rang while you were away and said that her room was ready and that she wanted her back.'

'What a pity! I love Sarah's company. Where is she now?'

'I've no idea,' said Seamus. 'Perhaps she's gone for a walk. She hasn't got to go back to London until tomorrow and I'm sure she'll want to sit next to you at dinner.'

* * *

The atmosphere in the dining room at dinner was eerie and filled with horrifying foreboding. None of the children were present. Hattie, Biddy, Eileen and Sean had been expelled from the house in turn. Paddy was in bed with a fever, and Shamie had left of his own accord because of the lingering disharmony and gloom in the house, even when Melissa was away.

O'Rafferty and Melissa sat at either end of the long,

dining-room table. The distance between them made the atmosphere even tenser for Sarah, who sat between them. Conversation did not come easily to Melissa, now that she was on the waggon, and her husband's fear that she might one day find out about his affair with his niece, depressed him and caused him to be equally silent.

Even the cook sensed the aura in the room and handed the dishes round the table with her head lowered, as if someone had died.

Sarah was the first to break the silence.

'Are you feeling a bit better, Aunt Melissa?'

'Yes, very much, thank you, Sarah.'

'I'm afraid my mother has finished redecorating my room in London and she wants me to go home tomorrow. I hate to have to go but I've booked my flight now.'

'I'm sorry you have to go. You're the only person in this miserable place who can make me laugh.'

This embarrassed Sarah. The last thing she wanted to hear was yet another description of an O'Rafferty row.

O'Rafferty sat looking down at the table. He didn't like the idea of being alone with Melissa, once Sarah had left. He thought of telling Eileen to come home. She had been banished from the house two weeks ago after a furious row in which her father had said that it was improper to wear false eyelashes.

The rest of the dinner continued in a strained silence, broken eventually by Melissa.

'I do hope you'll excuse me. I've got rather a nasty pain in my right side. Seamus, will you help me up to bed?'

O'Rafferty leapt from his chair, his face reddened with guilt. He and Sarah helped Melissa up, each taking an arm. He took his frail wife upstairs and lifted her into bed. She was about as heavy as a rag doll.

Once in bed, Melissa felt happier.

94

'I don't think I'll be up in time to see you go, Sarah, so we'll have to say "goodbye" now.'

Sarah sat on the bed and kissed her aunt. As her cheek crushed against Melissa's, a surge of revulsion went through her. She couldn't bear physical contact with the flesh that O'Rafferty had caressed.

'Goodbye, Aunt Melissa. It was very kind of you to put up with me for all these weeks. I've been so happy here.'

'Good,' said Melissa, rolling on to her left side to ease her pain. 'You've been a really good guest, best of the guests,' she added vaguely. By now, her eyes were closed. O'Rafferty ushered Sarah out.

* * *

O'Rafferty came down to breakfast at about eight-thirty the next morning and found his niece eating bacon and eggs.

'Hullo, Sare. I'm taking you to the airport. What time is your flight?'

'Check in's at nine fifty-five.'

'Is your suitcase ready?'

'Yes, everything's ready.' She deliberately avoided meeting her uncle's eyes as she felt she was about to cry.

'We must go in ten minutes, lassie. Don't cry. I told you I was coming to London.'

Once in the car, Sarah was convulsed with tears. O'Rafferty put his arm round her. 'You really must cheer up, lassie. You know I'm coming to London. I can't have you fussing like this. Your tears are spoiling your beauty.'

O'Rafferty drove fast and, in Sarah's opinion, dangerously. He swerved his Ford Capri round the narrow roads to Dublin Airport and overtook two buses on a blind bend. Sarah was so unhappy that she didn't care whether she would be fatally injured or not. She lay with her head on O'Rafferty's knee, soaking his clothes with her tears.

O'Rafferty pulled to a screeching halt in the underground part of Dublin's multi-storey car park.

'We've got plenty of time, lassie. Come on, let's get in the back.'

He scrambled over the seat and started to undress. He only removed the clothing necessary to make an act of sex possible.

Sarah climbed into the back and sat astride him.

'For God's sake don't scream, Sare, not this time,' muttered O'Rafferty.

They both took a long time to relieve themselves. Sarah felt much better, although a cloud of post-coital gloom descended on O'Rafferty. He got into the driver's seat.

'Come on, Sare. You must sit in front, otherwise passers-by will think I'm your bleeding chauffeur!'

'I must go, Uncle Seamus, I'll miss my plane.'

O'Rafferty caressed her mane of blonde, streaked hair. 'We've got a few minutes to go. I've got something very important to say.'

'Oh, I know, the third thing.'

'No, lassie, I can't tell you that yet. Listen carefully. In one week's time, you will meet me in the lobby of the Elizabeth Hotel in Elizabeth Street, London SW1 at exactly seven-thirty on the evening of 13 September. I have booked a double room there for a few days. I have booked under the name of James Fletcher and you will be referred to as Mrs Fletcher. Before we open any kind of conversation, you will approach me and use the following code.'

'What's all this?' Sarah interrupted irritably. 'Are you in some kind of trouble?'

'No, lassie! You're being silly.'

'Then what's all this for?'

'You'll understand when we go to bed. That's the right time and the right place for me to tell you the third thing.'

Sarah's sadness had dispersed and was replaced by a feeling of excitement and intrigue.

'All right, I'll be there. What's the code?'

'It's, "That dressing-gown looks pretty eccentric"!'

'Please, Uncle Seamus, don't make silly jokes at my expense. Will you be wearing a dressing-gown?'

'Yes, of course I'll be wearing a fockin' dressing-gown. How could you use that code if I wasn't?'

'All right, Uncle Seamus. I'll do as you say,' said Sarah fearfully.

As the plane pulled out along the tarmac, Sarah, who was sitting in a window seat, saw her uncle leaning over the balcony of the departure lounge. They saw each other for a fleeting second. Sarah saw him mouthing the words 'trust me', and once the plane was airborne, she ordered a large quantity of whisky with intent to get systematically drunk. She was relieved to be travelling by plane because she had been drinking too much over the weeks to be able to drive her car which she had left at Mulligan Manor.

*   *   *

She arrived at her parents' Westminster house inebriated. The first person she saw was Tessa, her mother.

'How dare you go away for so long without telephoning or writing!' shouted Tessa.

'I wrote twice,' lied Sarah. Although potentially violent and endowed with a horrific temper, she hated any kind of domestic scene with her own blood. She was incapable of arguing with her own blood because for some reason she thought that there was something incestuous about it.

'Perhaps you forgot to post your letters. If letters are not posted, they have a tendency not to arrive,' said Tessa.

'I did post them. In fact, I posted them myself. The O'Raffertys' phone was out of order and I could only get through via the Dublin operators. Whenever I got through to them, there was no answer your end.' This was another lie.

'Well, come on, aren't you interested in seeing your lovely, new room? It cost the earth to do.'

'Of course I am.'

The walls of Sarah's room had been painted in tortoiseshell, the interior equivalent of leopard skin. She and her mother shared a love of leopard skin.

'It looks absolutely wonderful!' said Sarah but her mind was on the act of sex she would soon be sharing with her uncle. She had bought a calendar at Heathrow Airport so that she could cross off the days until his visit to London.

The Elizabeth Hotel in Elizabeth Street was small and seedy. In its hall was a heavily stained, Persian carpet, frayed at the edges. The once white walls were filthy and even the act of repainting them would have achieved only a modicum of improvement.

Sarah arrived at seven o'clock in the evening, to make sure that she was in the right place. When she saw the gloomy hotel, she struggled to equate it with O'Rafferty's tastes in interior decoration. She wondered whether he had duped her for some incomprehensible reason and was not intending to turn up at all. Her eyes filled with tears. She had been thinking about his primitive technique as a lover for a whole week.

She sat down on a moth-eaten chair by the gas fire in the lobby, contemplating different methods of suicide. As she went through them, her mild gloom turned to despair. Swallowing pills? Not wise, she thought, as the person using this method often chokes to death. Hanging? She knew that she would be too incompetent to tie the noose correctly and would die of asphyxiation. She decided that flinging herself from a high building would be the best option – that is if O'Rafferty were to let her down.

'Can, I help you, madam?'

Until now, she had no idea that there was someone with her. In a dark alcove in the corner of the filthy-looking hall, sat a greasy-haired Arab who stank of foul-smelling incense. His left eye reminded her of Britbuster's eyes. It was diseased, its pupil covered with a gooey substance which looked like white glue and which suppurated every time he blinked. His broken, gold teeth looked like old, piano keys and his breath stank like a sewer.

The appearance of this man only increased Sarah's suspicions that this was the last hotel in London that her uncle would book himself into. Her suspicions increased her rage and her disgust at being in the presence of this repulsive-looking man.

'I asked you if I could help you,' repeated the Arab, without smiling.

Sarah deliberately looked away from him, to save herself from having to look at his leaking eye.

'If you want to help me, you can get me a glass of whisky, no ice, no water.'

The Arab took fifteen minutes to bring the drink. Sarah swallowed it in one gulp.

'Get me another!'

'What are you doing in this hotel?'

'I'm due to meet my husband here. I said, "Get me another"!'

'In my country, a woman would be stoned to death for drinking alcohol,' the Arab remarked, trying to catch Sarah's eye.

'You're not in your own bloody country now!' she shouted, now on the verge of tears. 'You're in this country. Get me another whisky.'

The Arab granted her request with extreme reluctance.

She paid him. Then she drank the second glass more slowly, and began to feel more peaceful as she warmed herself by the gas fire.

It was now seven-fifty p.m. and there was still no sign of O'Rafferty, with or without his dressing-gown.

Sarah strode over to the Arab.

'My husband's name is Mr Frazer. He's booked into this hotel-so-called. He promised to meet me here at seven-thirty. I'm worried because he hasn't arrived yet. Can you look through your book to check if he's made a reservation and get me another glass of whisky while you're at it.'

'Do you want the whisky first or the information?' asked the Arab disinterestedly.

'The whisky.'

'Have you ever heard of a word called "please"?'

'I don't feel like using it.'

This time, he asked her for her money in advance. The whisky was brought in and she drank it straight away.

'Mr Frazer? You must help me! Is he in your book?'

The Arab opened the dog-eared book and showed it to Sarah.

'No one's booked under that name,' he said.

Sarah must have gone temporarily insane. She rushed out into the street and started screaming, so that if O'Rafferty had failed to book in, he might at least be on his way and hear her. She clung to a lamp-post to steady herself.

'*That dressing-gown looks pretty eccentric! That dressing-gown looks pretty eccentric!*' She bellowed the words at least ten times until she felt as if her tonsils were bleeding. Passers-by, including a parson, who was out of his mind because he felt he was losing his faith, assumed that Sarah was mad and walked over to the other side of the street to avoid her.

She staggered back into the hotel.

The overbearing figure of Seamus O'Rafferty towered in front of her. He was wearing a full-length, leopard-skin tinted, bath-towel dressing-gown with a black, velvet strip at the bottom to cover his feet with.

'That dressing-gown looks pretty eccentric,' said Sarah quietly.

O'Rafferty embraced her. 'This mess-up is entirely your fault,' he said. 'I told you to ask for Mr Fletcher. Instead, you asked for Mr Frazer. Perhaps I am partly to blame because I was so tired after my flight that I fell asleep and wasn't woken in time to see you at seven-thirty. Apparently, you gave this poor lad a pretty bad time,' he added, pointing at the Arab. 'He said you were a bit rude to him.'

'I was desperate. I thought you weren't going to come.' In a lower voice, she added, 'He took no interest in my plight and was sullen and uncooperative.'

'All right, all right. Come up and see the modest room we'll be staying in. It's certainly better than nothing. I won't take long to dress. Then we'll go out to dinner.'

* * *

The restaurant was an uncrowded Angus Steakhouse in Victoria Street. O'Rafferty ushered his niece into a magenta, velvet-covered seat by the window and sat down beside her. They ordered claret, prawn cocktail and steak. O'Rafferty was unusually quiet but broke the silence after the first course.

'I'm a bit worried about you, Sarah. You don't seem to be capable of keeping your cool when things go wrong. If you can't learn to do that, our relationship is not going to work.'

Sarah took a large gulp of wine. She wondered to what extent her uncle knew of her behaviour while she was waiting for him.

'What do you mean, Uncle Seamus?'

101

'I can give an example of what I never knew to be your inability to be calm when difficulties arise. That man in the hall said you were very rude and odd because you couldn't find me, when you confused Fletcher with Frazer. He said you drank quite a lot of whisky and that you went out into the street, shouting that the dressing-gowns of passers-by were pretty eccentric. Who the hell would wear a dressing-gown in the fockin' street?'

Sarah was ashamed but nervously amused.

'I did it because I thought that there was some hope of your being upstairs, running late and that you might have heard me.'

'You should have obeyed my instructions. You should have sat quietly in the hall, reading a book, until I came. I stress again that if you had got the right name, the man in the hall would have come up and woken me. In other words, you showed extreme hysteria, lack of trust in my word, and incompetence. It must never happen again if you and I are to remain lovers.'

Sarah's immediate reaction was to blame the Arab who had described her to O'Rafferty. She was also deeply embarrassed, thinking that she had disappointed him.

'I'm sorry, Uncle Seamus,' she muttered. 'It will never happen again.'

'Good girl. A calm, cool, rational approach is going to be essential in your life. It is here that we come to the third thing which I promised to tell you about.'

Sarah laid her hand on her uncle's shoulder.

'When I do tell you the third thing, you might get a very nasty shock. You will then be faced with having to decide whether to leave me or to run away with me.'

'I've been in suspense for long enough. Tell me now.'

'No, lassie. It will have to be back in the hotel, after we've sported and lain, of course.'

Back in the hotel, O'Rafferty courteously said, 'goodnight'

to the Arab and guided his drunken niece upstairs. He dragged off her jeans and blue and white striped T-shirt, crushing his mouth against hers. Then, with her assistance, he took off his own clothes which were just as informal as hers.

'Go down on me, lassie, for God's sake!'

Once sufficiently excited, he pushed her gently on top of the bed and performed the act in the savage, primitive manner that she craved. She got into bed, unceremoniously wiping herself clean on the cheap, cotton sheet, while he got in beside her and let her head rest on his chest.

'I am ready now, my pretty, little niece.' His face appeared strange and white. He looked older. 'I'm afraid I've got to tell you the third thing.'

His repeated promises to tell her the third thing made Sarah unpleasantly tense each time. She had no idea what he was going to tell her and the more she thought about it, the worse she thought it would be.

'All right,' she said, 'but I'll need some whisky first.'

O'Rafferty put on his dressing-gown and went downstairs to order a bottle of whisky. The Arab brought the tray to the room. O'Rafferty and Sarah knocked back two glasses.

'OK, Uncle Seamus,' she began, once they were both in bed, 'let's hear the third thing.'

'I work for the IRA,' he said huskily. 'I'm a senior cell commander, that is to say the commander of a cell of four people including myself.'

'You? You what?'

O'Rafferty looked unusually agitated.

'I knew this would hurt you, lassie, because you come from a prestigious, British family. You must make your decision by tomorrow morning – whether to stay with me and help us – or to go back to your family.'

Sarah's three siblings had all moved out of her parents' house and she had no job. She would sit in her room, reading the newspapers most days. On other days, she would go to the cinema. She would have lunch in a pub and spend the afternoons educating herself, either in the London library or in the National Gallery. In the evenings, she would play the piano. Her visits to the National Gallery gave her no pleasure because she had no interest in art, and only forced herself to learn about it to show off her knowledge to others, and to keep up with her elder sister, Miranda, an art historian who, in the past, had taunted her about her ignorance.

On the other hand, Sarah was very musical. She spent a lot of her time listening to classical music, her preferences being for Beethoven's Ninth Symphony, Mozart's operas, Bizet's *Carmen* and Verdi's *La Traviata*. She had a sizeable repertoire of airs to play on the piano and was able knock out a reasonable *Für Elise* and *Moonlight Sonata*.

When Miranda had chided her about her ignorance about art, which she did on one occasion when she showed Sarah a photograph of Donatello's *David*, and asked her who had sculpted it, Sarah retorted, 'Perhaps you'd care to tell me who wrote the *Sarabande Duo* in D minor.'

Sarah never liked to be outsmarted. If a conversation were taking place about a historical event of which she knew nothing, she would remain silent and would go straight to the library to familiarize herself.

The family she hailed from was a highly literary family. Sarah also liked to keep up with one of her brothers, Selwyn, who knew many Shakespeare speeches by heart. Sarah herself had been made to learn a lot of Shakespeare's speeches, due to her myriad of misdemeanours as a child. If Selwyn recited a speech of which Sarah only remembered the first ten lines, she would go to her room and make sure that she learnt the rest of it.

'You're very quiet, lassie,' said O'Rafferty. 'What are you thinking about?'

'I was just thinking about leaving my family for you. They are all fiercely competitive, particularly about cultural knowledge. Sometimes, it's so tiring. What I need is a job.'

'There won't be any problem there,' said O'Rafferty. 'If you do make up your mind to work in a cell with me as the commander, you will find that the other cell members will be earning their living during the day as well. What sort of job do you want?'

'I want to train to be a medical secretary.'

'That's a funny thing for a girl to want to do. Why do you want to do that?'

'Because, being petrified of illness and death, I have a morbid fascination for both of them. I'd love to be in an office surrounded by bustling, white-coated doctors, with stretchers being rushed along the corridors. Also, I like the smells in hospitals. They remind me of my school.'

O'Rafferty lit a cigarette. 'Sure, you're an eccentric young girl, lassie! Can you type?'

'Yes.'

'Then you don't need to train. All you have to do is get a few medical textbooks from a library and learn how to spell the words you're not familiar with. By the way – how do your spell "cirrhosis"?'

'S-I-R-R-O-S-I-S.'

'Wrong. Even I know how to spell it and I'm only a farmer. I suggest you get up early each morning, having bought an alphabetical notebook, go to the library, ask for books about every part of the body and learn the words. Once you've done that, you can make up some imaginary doctor's notepaper and let me do you a reference. I don't have to know anything about medicine to use my common sense.'

'How long will you be in London?' asked Sarah suddenly.

'My bosses have sent me here for six months. You'll be able to be a medical secretary in London during that period. Then you can come back with me and work in Dublin.'

'Where does Melissa come in on all this? Does she know that you work for the IRA?'

O'Rafferty hated being asked that question. It gave him no pleasure to discuss a woman with whom he was in love, with another woman he was equally in love with.

'Yes, she knows, lassie. She's known all along. She has come to accept it, as long as I don't harm her brothers and sisters. She's coming to London tomorrow and will stay here for six months. For the first week, she's chosen to stay at the Savoy. As you know, she has inherited an enormous fortune. Then she's moving into a rented flat and I shall have to spend the afternoons with her, and tell her that I work all night for the cause. Most of her brothers and sisters live in London. She likes seeing them and I think the change of air will do her good.'

Sarah was fed up with hearing about her rival's domestic arrangements and changed the subject.

'I'm very confused, Uncle Seamus.'

'Why, lassie?'

'It's true that my politics are, because of my personality, anarchic, which is why I vote Tory. I believe that party to be the closest party to anarchy that one can get. It is true that my love for you has blinded my intellect. I am roused by all those rebel songs you used to make me sing as a child. I have read a bit about Irish history as well as being taught by you. I know that the Irish have historically had a raw deal and that Catholics in Belfast are sometimes persecuted. Do you actually want me to work for the IRA?'

'I'm not a bully. You don't have to do so against your will, but you must understand that the organization is the only one strong enough to get the British out of Ulster, and that can't be achieved without continuous violence.

Of course, if your conscience prevents you from wishing to help us, it would put quite a strain on our relationship. Remember, I will never force you to do anything against your will, but if our different convictions forced us to separate, it would break my heart.'

Sarah went quiet. O'Rafferty said, 'I have reason to believe that you disliked your childhood, Sarah. You are proud and bitter. Come on, tell me. That's the way to get it out of your system.'

Part III

Childhood and Adolescence of Sarah

Sarah Lloyd was not like other women. She felt that fate had treated her badly. She was staunchly loyal to her loved ones, but exceptionally vicious and vindictive towards those who wounded her or besmirched the honour of her loved ones, by slighting either them or herself. While being capable of extreme compassion towards those she loved, Sarah was cold, calculating, devoid of conscience and had a psychopathic streak.

She believed that charity began at home and ended there. When watching news bulletins portraying piteous famines in Third World countries, she was indifferent and was even heard to suggest mass genocide on the grounds that victims of starvation had nothing to live for.

She had five nephews in all, and spoiled them rotten, being a soppy, doting and indulgent aunt who denied them nothing.

Sarah had an obsessive and overtly possessive personality. She felt that she had had a heinously unhappy childhood and that she had the right to avenge herself in adulthood. A key factor in her savage resentment of mankind in general, had been the marriage of her eldest brother, Selwyn, who had married when she was fourteen. He had married an Australian woman and had emigrated to Australia. From an early age, Sarah had hero-worshipped her handsome brother and even thought that she was in love with him.

She would run errands for him, wash his clothes, massage his shoulders, sew on buttons, make his bed, turn the bedclothes down for him in the evenings and even put the toothpaste on his brush for him. When she wasn't lovingly performing these 'duties', she spent all her spare time desperately trying to equal Selwyn's intellect.

Within the Lloyd family, it was not uncommon for many of its members to immerse themselves in the written word. Whenever Sarah came into the library, she found Selwyn bashing a typewriter with a vengeance. He would continue for up to three hours at a time without getting into deadlock.

Sarah was twelve at the time. She and Selwyn were in the library in the Lloyds' country house in Buckinghamshire. She went up to him and put her hands on his shoulders.

'What are you writing, Selwyn?'

'A thriller about British agents landing in the middle of Moscow, disguised as astronauts from another planet. Want to have a look at what I've done so far?'

'Oh, yes. It's an honour to have a brother who is so good-looking and so clever.'

Selwyn laughed and slapped his thigh.

'You're right, little sister. Go upstairs to my bedroom and put a notice on my door, saying, *"I've got a damned good figure and I'm devilishly handsome"*.'

'Of course I'll do that for you. Then I'll come back.'

When she returned, Sarah sat by Selwyn's side, reading his manuscript. She thought what an original idea it was, only capable of being engineered by Selwyn's genius. Then she went quiet. She had had such a bad report the last term that her parents were incensed.

Against *Religious Knowledge*, was a short comment saying, 'Isaiah would turn in his grave'. Against *Gymnastics* was: 'I cannot assess Sarah's prowess as a gymnast, since I only see her lying flat on her back, determined to do nothing at all except giggle when I am obliged to utter the words, "This is just not good enough".'

As a punishment, Sarah's father, Sir Alec Lloyd, told her that she was to write a book, about fifteen thousand words long, on the subject of her choice. She chose to write a thriller about the Berlin Wall. Much serious confusion between communist and capitalist lifestyles was shown in Sarah's bold, ambitious, if perplexing prose.

The story was set in the 1960s and described two eighteen-year-old, East German lovers by the extraordinary names of Eva Fitzownhearse and Andy Slapstick, who was a postman. Both lovers were trying to escape to the West in a truck with two javelins roped to its bonnet and, even more unbelievably, flame throwers which covered twenty yards.

Sarah's confusion was at its worst when, just to cover space to fill in the fifteen thousand words, she had elaborately written about Herr Slapstick's bathroom. She had described it as a marble chamber with a sunken bath the size of a swimming pool, filled to the brim with perfumed asses' milk.

'Do you really think that a postman living in East Berlin in the 1960s could afford to bathe in a sunken bath filled with perfumed asses' milk?' Sir Alec asked her in a moment of baffled confusion.

Yet another of Sarah's mistakes was to describe the overgrown garden outside the tenement flat block that her heroine had lived in. The grisly caretaker was accounted for as being 'too idle to appoint a gardener'.

In addition, Herr Slapstick, who came to the heroine's flat to take her out to discuss the escape, rode an underfed stallion, allegedly stolen from a zoo. Herr Slapstick and Fraulein Fitzownhearse would gallop through the bare, littered streets of East Berlin, both astride this wretched steed.

Sarah thought about her book, wondering if Selwyn would like it.

'You're very quiet all of a sudden, little sister. Is something wrong?'

'No, not wrong. I'm writing a book as well. It's a thriller about the Berlin Wall.'

'Well, go and get it and I'll read it. I understand you had a very bad report last term. Mummy and Daddy were in an art gallery when they read it. Your French report just said one single word, "*Merde!*" They both fainted simultaneously.'

Sarah liked Selwyn's sense of humour.

'Were there any exclamation marks after "*merde*"?'

'Yes, ten!' shouted Selwyn. 'Come on, show me your book.'

Sarah brought the book to Selwyn, hoping with all her heart that he would like it. He suggested that they go out to lunch together. He pointed out the various errors but was impressed by the plot.

'Carry on writing, little sister. You've got the gift. I'll make a pact with you. When we're both dead, we'll be as famous as the Brontë sisters.'

That day was one of the happiest days of Sarah's life. Selwyn had found out that she could write and respected her for it.

There had been an earlier incident in her life when Sarah was eight years old. It was just after Christmas and the snow was thick on the ground. Selwyn was about fifteen.

He came into his sister's room, carrying a toboggan.

'I'm going to give you the time of your life, little sister. Hurry up and get dressed. After you've had breakfast, I'm going to take you somewhere and you're going to love it.'

Selwyn held his small sister's hand and walked with her across the fields. He led her to the top of a long, steep hill.

112

'Come on, get on to the back of the toboggan and hold on to me.'

Sarah obeyed and Selwyn directed the toboggan down the hill which was so steep that it reached a speed of about forty m.p.h. Instinctively, Sarah dug her heels into the ground, fearing that she would get hurt if they didn't slow down.

They reached the bottom of the hill.

'You spoiled our ride!' shouted Selwyn in a rage.

'I was frightened,' said Sarah.

'Go home, coward!'

'Go home? Why?'

'Because you're a coward. I don't play games with cowards.'

Sarah stared at her elder brother in amazement.

'Are you deaf? I told you to go home. I told you I don't play with cowards.'

Sarah was so ashamed of being called a coward by the brother she worshipped, that she forced herself not to cry, even in the privacy of her own room. Instead, she looked at her face in the mirror and uttered abuse at herself and finally vowed to herself that she would never again in her life show either fear or cowardice.

The following day, she took the toboggan to the same place alone. This time, she did not dig her heels into the ground and came back to the house to find Selwyn.

'I did it this time, Selwyn. I didn't dig my heels into the ground, so I'm not a coward any more.'

'I'll come out this afternoon and see for myself,' said Selwyn.

This time Sarah got it right.

'That's much better, little sister. You're getting braver.'

These words were an elixir to Sarah. Her self-confidence grew and she became cheekier and cockier.

When Selwyn married a willowy, blonde, Australian

113

woman, Sarah became sadder and sadder, but her pride forced her to suppress her sorrow and she became cold, ruthless and violent. It was about a year after Selwyn's marriage and emigration to Australia that an illness diagnosed as schizophrenia descended on Sarah and she was forcibly committed.

Sarah had another brother, Mivart, who was devoted to her. When she was institutionalized, Mivart, sometimes accompanied by Sarah's lively cousin, Varinia, would give Sarah hope for the future and make her laugh. Indeed, Mivart's extreme loyalty and love for his sister made her feel more adjusted as the days went by.

Mivart had become the financial correspondent of the Lloyds' family newspaper. His work had led him to meet Sir Jasper Montrose, a glamorous, somewhat controversial businessman and publisher of newspapers and scientific journals. Mivart had introduced Sarah to Sir Jasper and she had fallen in love with him at first sight. It was Sir Jasper who barged into the mental institution in which Sarah was incarcerated and physically carried her away.

Sarah remained in love with Sir Jasper until one tragic night a long time hence, when he died at sea.

She decided to tell her uncle about the two men she had murdered in her teens. One of them was constantly harassing her, both psychologically and physically when she rejected his love. They were on the fourteenth floor of the Hilton Hotel in Park Lane. The lovesick man was leaning out of the window weeping. Sarah, then aged sixteen, went to his side, pretending to comfort him, but gave him a hard push, causing him to spatter the pavement below.

The tears were still on the dead man's cheeks. The verdict was suicide. Sarah felt no remorse, no shame and no regret, because the man was not her beloved Selwyn.

The second murder was a different case. Sarah was

eighteen. The man she loved, whom she had met in a hospital that she had worked in as a receptionist, was a junior doctor who had left her for someone else. A Christmas party was taking place. The doctor and his new love were kissing passionately at the top of a spiral staircase descending for three storeys in the hospital's morbid anatomy museum. Pickled human organs floated in jars on all the shelves, fuelling Sarah's fascination for death.

The assembled company were getting progressively drunk, including Sarah and the doomed couple. By now, the junior doctor was moving his hand up and down his new girlfriend's thighs as she threw back her head, making gurgling noises.

Sarah walked towards them and pretended to trip in their direction in her high-heeled shoes. They both lost their balance and fell to their deaths. No one was blamed. The coroner concluded that the deaths were due to accidental causes.

* * *

O'Rafferty held Sarah close to him as he listened to all her stories, including the last two which she thought would give him the impression of cold-blooded toughness. She knew that, to be associated with the IRA, one had to have no regard whatever for human life and that only those in this category would be acceptable.

Part IV

O'Rafferty and Sarah Again

'I may have left something out, but that's roughly the story of my life,' said Sarah.

'What have you left out?' asked O'Rafferty.

'Well, I'm very vindictive. If someone wrongs me I pay them back.'

'Give an example.'

'I was working as a hospital receptionist when Sir Jasper Montrose died at sea. My boss was jealous of my love for him and sacked me when I was grieving. 'To repay him, I sent taxi drivers and deliverers of pizzas round to his house every fifteen minutes of the night. I also sent the National Front, the British National Party and the Communist Party to his house – just by writing letters in his name, saying that he wished to join these parties. I sent a rodent inspector to his house late at night and a Jehovah's witness too. When you send the Communist Party round to someone's house, they don't do any harm but they're a dreadful nuisance. They're like a lot of wasps buzzing round and round a plate. They stay for hours and won't go away.

'I also rang Customs and Excise at Heathrow Airport, and said that the boss was carrying heroin and crack cocaine rectally. In addition, I booked an alarm call for four-thirty a.m. Finally, I sent him anonymous leaflets about impotence, premature ejaculation and erectyle dysfunction.

117

'As far as he is concerned, I think that's the lot. I believe, not in an eye for an eye and a tooth for a tooth; I believe in an eye for a tooth and a limb for an eye.'

'Jaysus, Sarah,' said O'Rafferty, 'I hope I don't ever get on the wrong side of you! Your suffering has made you tough. You're ideal fodder for the IRA.

'Where your family is concerned, I know Selwyn, Miranda and Mivart well. They're very noisy like yourself. I think Selwyn and you are most alike – you're both so fockin' eccentric. I remember Selwyn crashing into the backs of other cars by accident and shouting to their owners, "How dare you reverse into me! I'm a magistrate and I'll give you a stiff sentence when you appear before my bench!"'

O'Rafferty and Sarah lay silent for a while. Sarah fell asleep but O'Rafferty woke her abruptly.

'You mentioned Sir Jasper Montrose?'

'Yes. What of it? Did you ever meet him?'

'I've heard of him. He was very famous. No, I never met him.'

'Why did you suddenly raise the subject?' asked Sarah.

O'Rafferty put both his hands on Sarah's shoulders. His facial expression was one of sorrow and humiliation. 'Because you said how attracted to him you were, and if I ever hear you mention his name again, I think I will die of jealousy.'

'All right. I won't mention his name again,' said Sarah.

O'Rafferty went to sleep but Sarah felt unsettled and had insomnia that night. She thought about her uncle's wish for her to work for the IRA as an alternative to damaging their affair.

She remembered the murders she had committed in cold blood and after some brooding and bitter thoughts about her childhood, a wave of self-centred anger surged through her. She was convinced that she could murder anyone in cold blood at her uncle's command, and she prepared herself to carry out any order he gave her, provided her victims were not dear to her. Her love for her uncle was so intense that she made a decision to obey him implicitly. 'And why not?' she asked herself. Perhaps the Catholics in Northern Ireland really had had a raw deal, although this aspect of her decision played only a minor part in her reasoning.

Sarah tapped her sleeping uncle on the shoulder. He woke up with a start and instinctively reached for his walking stick (carried to give an impression of respectability) which he mistook for his rifle.

'For God's sake, lassie, not now. I've been running around all day and I need my sleep.'

'Uncle Seamus, I've been awake all night thinking about your proposal.'

'Yes?'

'Ireland's had it rough,' Sarah began banally. 'I'm going to help you and I'm not going back on my word. There's one thing I do ask, though, and that is that you will keep your promise and let me be in the same cell of which you are the commander.'

'That's just what I've thought out. One of the volunteers in my cell was lifted not so long ago. Congratulations on making the right decision. There is one last thing, though.'

'What?'

'You're going to have to shed that upper class, English accent of yours and sharpish.'

'To be sure I will. I won't be letting you down, b'fockin' Jaysus!'

O'Rafferty was about to go back to sleep when Sarah interrupted him.

'There's just one more thing, Uncle Seamus.'

'What?' he replied irritably.

'What about my family? They're not IRA targets, are they?'

'No!' shouted Seamus. 'The movement's only interested in what concerns Ireland, not bloody writers and journalists. I'd be obliged if you'd let me get some sleep.'

In the morning, they fornicated again, before asking the diseased-looking Arab, who had slept behind his desk, to bring them bread and coffee. They rolled over and lay on their backs.

'What is it, Uncle Seamus? What are you looking so haunted for?' asked Sarah.

O'Rafferty was staring at the ceiling, his grey eyes furtively moving from one area to another. He grabbed his niece by the arm, inadvertently hurting her.

'Did you do this with that fellow, Montrose?' he asked vehemently.

'We've already made an agreement not to discuss him,' said Sarah, 'and if I can stick to that agreement, so can you.'

O'Rafferty was still not satisfied. He knew that he had a lot in common with Sir Jasper Montrose, namely a tendency to bully his children, a short-fuse personality, fierce and ambitious convictions and, above all, similar, rugged, good looks.

He decided that he wouldn't raise the subject with Sarah again for fear of losing her, but the image of the Cossack-like, swashbuckling publisher was to haunt his dreams as well as his waking thoughts for the rest of his life.

All he wanted to know was whether Sarah had had carnal relations with him. Even if she said that she had, it would have been better than not knowing at all.

* * *

Sarah bought herself a typewriter, practised her typing and made herself familiar with medical terminology, to enable her to enrol at an agency and get a temporary, medical, secretarial job in a hospital. Such work was highly paid at the time because the wages of permanent secretaries were too low to attract applicants. In addition, rather than face her parents, she had written to them, saying that she had been offered a well-paid job outside London, and had moved into a flat with two other girls whose telephone had been cut off because they hadn't paid the bill. She said she was sorry about being unable to use her newly-decorated room but she had to put her career first. She added that she would write home regularly.

'Once you've settled down in a hospital, you're going to feel more secure emotionally,' said O'Rafferty, who had suspected over the few days spent in London, that his niece had seemed lost and even frightened of doing the work that would be expected of her in the evenings and at weekends.

'It's a shame that you have to go to work, but I can't really see your parents continuing to give you an allowance, not after you've left home in such a hurry, without spending much time in the room they've had decorated for you. If one of my brats had done that, I'd have given them a fockin', good thrashing and turned them out on to the streets. But I know you've done all this for old Seamus and, by God, I love you for it,' O'Rafferty told Sarah, adding, 'We're going to stay here for a couple of weeks until you feel a bit more stable. Then I'm taking somewhere else in London – not a hotel. I can't tell you where yet.'

'What address do I get my wages sent to?'

'You will demand payment in cash. Say you haven't got a bank account.'

They stayed in the seedy hotel for a fortnight. Because of the fortune O'Rafferty had accrued through the winning of his racehorses over the years, he didn't have to go to work, except when he was on his farm where he worked through pleasure and not necessity. Like himself, his father and grandfather had been staunch republicans as well as shrewd racehorse breeders and, like O'Rafferty, they had contributed handsomely to republican funds.

* * *

O'Rafferty and Sarah were dining at the poorly-frequented steakhouse in Victoria Street which they visited every evening. Sarah had been dreading what her uncle was about to say during their two-week stay in London.

'We'll have to arrange for you to be trained as a volunteer for the IRA,' O'Rafferty said casually, having observed that his niece had already drunk half a bottle of red wine, although she hadn't yet finished her prawn cocktail.

'I knew that was coming sooner or later, Uncle Seamus,' said Sarah in a tone of apprehension and gloom. 'I'll hate being away from you with a lot of strangers.'

'Come on lassie! The training's not going to last for ever. You know very well that you'll be doing this for me. Besides, you've got a nice, lively nature about you. You'll make friends quite easily. I only hope that you don't fall in love with a man of your own age.'

Sarah pushed the remainder of her prawn cocktail round in circles with her spoon.

'What will this training entail and where will it take place?' she asked.

'The IRA has been using an old farm for training volunteers,' said O'Rafferty. 'It's in the middle of nowhere in County Wexford. They train you to handle guns and make explosive devices. Here's what you're not going to like. They also train you in physical fitness and you'll be made to complete obstacle courses, just like in any other army.'

Sarah didn't mind so much about being taught to kill and maim civilians unknown to her, but there was nothing she hated more than the obligation to perform gymnastic feats. At school, she was ironically nicknamed 'British Bullet'. Indeed, she never took any physical exercise and preferred to spend her spare time, when alone, going to cinemas and sitting at home playing the piano.

As she had been born and bred in London, the countryside and even the picturesque walks it offered, depressed her. When she wasn't with her uncle, she only felt at ease amidst concrete buildings.

The melancholy expression on his niece's face, unchanged over a period of ten minutes in silence, jolted O'Rafferty. The fear crossed his mind that Sarah no longer wanted to go through with any involvement with the IRA, which would have irretrievably damaged the relationship that meant so much to him.

Like all fervent and committed republicans, O'Rafferty saw the cause as coming before any woman, however much he loved her, although the pain of losing Sarah would have been the equivalent of losing an arm or a leg in the fight for his beloved Green.

'You look as if the end of the world had come, lassie. If you want to back out, I shan't hold it against you but it will mean the end of our affair.'

Sarah poured herself a fifth glass of wine and drank it in one gulp. As the wine flowed through her system, her fear dispersed and her sense of intrigue stimulated her.

'It's not the training I mind,' she said, her speech slurred. 'It's the fitness and gymnastics I'm dreading. I was never any good at physical fitness at school. I can't shin up ropes or climbing frames. I can't even walk for so much as a mile without getting pains in my chest. It's not the guns and bombs I mind. It's being asked to run. Even when I was little, my mother said I needed exercise. Once we were out driving in the car and there was this idiotic jogger running along the pavement in the pouring rain.

'"Oh, can't we stop and put you outside to jog along with this man, darling?" my mother said. "Can't you go to a gym to keep fit?" She made me walk and walk and walk and she put me off exercise for life.'

O'Rafferty laughed uproariously.

'I think she was right, lassie. If you don't take exercise, you'll get flabby and unhealthy. Jaysus, girl, considering the way you perform between the sheets, I'd never have suspected you of being unfit.'

* * *

Three of the trainees on the desolate farm in the heart of County Wexford were the children of some of O'Rafferty's closest comrades. Their fathers had been trained in the same camp as he was.

He took the ferry, accompanied by Sarah, and drove her to the farm. He introduced her as his niece, Sarah Conlon, and said that she had been brought up as an adopted member of his family, as her own parents had been shot dead by RUC agents.

Sarah's Irish accent had been cultivated to perfection. Her long, blonde hair, combined with her green T-shirt and matching tight, green jeans, automatically turned the heads of two other trainees, Finbar and Patrick, both dedicated, hate-filled, young men who were identical twins.

The twins shook hands with Sarah, entranced by her beguiling smile which was soon wiped from her face when she was shown the accommodation.

There was no central heating in the abandoned farmhouse and no running water either. The only way to carry water to the premises was to take two buckets to a nearby reservoir every day and bring them back, using a medieval milkmaid's yoke. The trainees would take it in turns to perform this arduous task. Hot food was not consumed on the premises, due to the absence of cooking facilities.

124

Instead, the trainees survived on pickled foods, tins of marinated fruit and other substances bought in stocks. Alcohol was not permitted on the farm, although the trainees were allowed to go to a local pub two miles away, which was safe because of the landlord's republican connections.

When Finbar showed Sarah the sleeping quarters, she saw before her an array of sleeping bags on a cold, stone floor, touching each other so that their occupants could gain what little warmth they could by physical contact.

Apart from Finbar and Patrick, there were two girls on the farm called Sheila and Bernadette. Sheila was a tall brunette who wore a large, silver cross over her navy blue tracksuit. Bernadette was a short, plump redhead with an irritating and persistent giggle. The twins, Finbar and Patrick, had slit, probing, green eyes, thick, black hair swept back showing widow's peaks, high cheekbones and beards.

Sarah wept silently throughout her first night on the farm. She felt wretched without her uncle but as the days went by, a part of the training programme gave her pleasure. Her favourite part of the course was target practice. She stunned the other trainees by her unusually skilled marksmanship with a rifle. She won the affection of the twins by her apparent loathing of the British, her ability to sing a number of Irish rebel songs, and above all the tightness of her jeans, which clung to her behind and set their blood on fire.

When it came to physical training, which entailed climbing over obstacles, Sarah was miserable. Sometimes she would ask for a break and secrete herself in a lavatory, smoke cigarettes and weep silently for her uncle.

The training course was run by a muscular, handsome-looking thug, known as B.K.K., an abbreviation for Brit-killer Kes. Where political issues were concerned, Kes was ruthless to the point of blatant sadism. He had once engineered the abduction of a British soldier from a Belfast street and had ordered his fingernails to be wrenched off and his tongue to be cut out.

Kes was more affable towards his trainees, however, and although he barked at them continuously, he gave them credit where credit was due. He had taken a liking to Sarah because she was a source of merriment to the team in off-duty hours and he respected her for her skill with a rifle.

'You're fockin unfit, Sarah Conlon!' he bawled at her one morning as she struggled up makeshift, rope ladders with tears on her cheeks. 'Sure, you won't be stopping for one of your rests either. You're not resting till you've finished the exercises.'

At the top of the rope ladder was a higher level on which there was a fifteen-foot high vaulting horse, similar to the one in the gym at Sarah's school. A rope hanging from a hook on the ceiling served as her only way of getting herself over the vaulting horse. Kes could see how hard she was trying.

'You'll be getting over that thing, Sarah Conlon,' he shouted, 'even if it takes you all night. I know you can do it. I can see the will in your face.'

Sarah climbed downwards on the rope ladder to give herself enough leverage to swing herself over the vaulting horse with the rope. As she swung her weight towards it, her leg collided with it and caused her so much pain that she fell into the empty space between the vaulting horse and the rope ladder.

Kes rushed over to her.

'Ah, come on now, Sarah Conlon. Are you hurt?'

'No. It was only a bang. I know I'm never going to get this right.'

Kes noticed the tears in her eyes. They were not tears

of pain but of misery through being without O'Rafferty. She knew that if she abandoned her training he would think less of her and probably ditch her.

'It's all right, Sarah. You know you're going to do it. If fat, little Bernadette can do it, I know you can.'

The warm words of encouragement from perhaps the cruellest operator in the entire IRA, only increased Sarah's tears. She made up her mind to satisfy him.

'I'm going to do it over and over again until I get it right, Kes!' she said sycophantically, so great was her determination to please him and thereby enable a favourable report to be passed on to O'Rafferty.

'That's my girl! Once you get it right, I'll buy you a jar.'

A streak of confused masochism surged through Sarah. In the back of her mind lurked the memory of her having lost her first love, namely her brother, who had emigrated to Australia, followed shortly afterwards by her committal to a mental institution.

In order to assuage her rage and self-pity, she yearned to cause herself even more physical pain, pretending she was inflicting it on mankind. She climbed on to the rope ladder a second time, this time retreating further to improve her leverage. She dragged the rope with her, hurled her weight at the vaulting horse and threw herself over it before letting go of the rope. She sprained her ankle, but the more it hurt the more her hatred towards the world in general was stimulated.

Kes ran over to her a second time.

'You've been as good as gold, Sarah Conlon, and you've hurt your foot into the bargain. Are you sure you're OK?'

'Sure, I'm OK. I'm so pleased I've mastered it. My foot hurts a bit but it'll pass.'

'Of course it will! Tonight we'll take you out to The Old Harp for a jar, eh?'

Sarah cheered up for she was invariably enraptured by an audience, irrespective of its quality.

'That sounds great, Kes. Jaysus, I could do with a few drinks. Then I can silence the place with my singing.'

Kes put his arm round her, knowing that she was going to sing her repertoire of rebel songs which her uncle had taught her.

'You're a rare girl, Sarah Conlon! We'll make a full-blooded, Irish heroine of you yet, daughter!'

Sarah stared Kes in the eye, her sycophancy and inordinate vanity forcing themselves into a stupefying cocktail of nausea.

'Oh, Kes, I don't just want to be a heroine. I want to be a martyr too and to bathe the Irish history books with my blood.'

Had Kes been fractionally more intuitive, he would have seen Sarah as being too good to be true. Instead, he looked into her face with love in his eyes and kissed her.

'Oh, come on now, Kes! Save your kisses until we get a united Ireland!'

Kes was not a man with a sense of humour but on this occasion he let out a lukewarm chuckle.

'A rare girl, eh! That's what you are, a rare girl!'

Sarah became progressively drunk that night in The Old Harp, and her comrades ordered her to stand on the counter and sing which she did raucously, revelling in the attention of her audience, like a cat guzzling a saucer of cream.

Back at the camp, Sarah put in her diaphragm and embarked on a flirtation with one of the twins, not knowing one from the other. Before the night was over, she had had both of them, pretending on each occasion that she was having sex with her uncle. She had talked incessantly throughout each sexual encounter about her scanty knowledge of the history of Ireland, occasionally breaking into song during the climax.

The team went to The Old Harp every evening at the end of the training sessions and Sarah's audience-craving behaviour continued and increased. Even the team members, who had been entranced by her wit and apparent gutsy dedication to the cause, began to get bored with her monopoly of the conversation and her persistently repetitive singing, which she threw herself into without being asked to do so. The landlord of the pub, himself an IRA member, who had once blown up a soldier's truck in London, was beginning to find the pretty, lively recruit, a 'fockin' bore'.

The final part of the training course entailed setting up explosive devices. This took place in a farmyard which was ideal for this purpose, due to the space it offered, reducing the risk of accidents. The trainees were being taught how to make hand grenades. Although Sarah was academically, musically and to some extent socially accomplished, she was far from being mechanically minded.

During one drill session, Kes ordered Finbar to throw a hand grenade, made by Sarah, at the gate dividing the farmyard from a field. It failed to explode. Sarah picked it up and tested it with her teeth. Aware that she had incompetently set up the grenade, she started to kick it along the ground like a ball, singing yet again.

'Sarah, what the fockin' hell are you doing?' yelled Kes. 'I'll come over and pick it up and dispose of it.'

The trainees watched motionless as Sarah continued to kick the grenade, certain it would not explode and determined to remain the centre of attention.

Kes cautiously picked it up and as he did so, it blew his arm off.

* * *

129

The team were not overtly sorry when O'Rafferty came to collect his niece after she had completed her training, but they were unanimous in praising her patriotism, her liveliness and her beauty.

'I hear you kept a pretty high profile on your training course, lassie,' O'Rafferty commented mildly as he drove Sarah in his Ford Capri to the ferry bound for England.

Sarah didn't answer. She was pleased to be back with her uncle but she missed the large audience which she craved.

'You're unusually quiet. I had a long talk with the people you trained with, including the instructor who blew his arm off. He said that you didn't stop talking for the whole time you were there. He also complained that you showed off all the time. You were forever frolicking and larking about, seeking attention.'

'I'll have you know that I broke my leg during the physical bit, and I did it all for you!' shouted Sarah.

'Now, come on, lassie. You know fockin' well you didn't break your leg. You sprained your ankle. Let's have a little less of your amateur dramatics.'

Sarah burst into tears.

'I didn't mean to hurt your feelings, lassie,' said O'Rafferty. 'A lot of the things you did at the camp, you did very well. I think they liked having you there,' he said, his voice softening, adding, 'well for the first few days at any rate.'

Sarah laughed quietly through her tears. O'Rafferty continued.

'Apparently, you learned a great deal on the course and you also worked very hard. However, if you are going to work under me as cell commander, you've got to keep a low profile. Do you not realize that fooling around, attracting attention is going to get you noticed, which you can't afford to be?

'I can just imagine you getting instructions to bomb a soldiers' barracks in London. I wouldn't put it past you to go up to a policeman and say, "The IRA has asked me to blow this barracks up. Where would be the best place for me to leave my carrier bag with the gelignite in it?"'

Sarah laughed hysterically and her laughter mingled with her tears.

'I'll try and do better, Uncle Seamus, I promise.'

O'Rafferty signalled for the vehicle behind him to overtake him. He held Sarah's hand.

'I know you will, lassie. All I'm saying is you mustn't talk so much all the time or make so much noise either. When you're working in the cell, that is when you're not earning, you will please put on an act of being shy and quiet; just be sweet, attentive and demure. Don't speak to anyone unless they speak to you first and please, for the holy love of Mike, don't sing to anyone unless specifically instructed to do so.'

'All right, Uncle Seamus,' said Sarah. The intensive course and absence of proper beds had exhausted her. She leant over and fell asleep on her uncle's knee.

* * *

O'Rafferty was under orders to reactivate a 'sleeping unit' in two rented rooms in Whitechapel, where he had been posted for six months. He and Sarah occupied one small room which had the welcome addition of an imitation, gas-operated fire, whose flames brightened the room by flickering throughout the night.

The other room was occupied by two trained volunteers, a couple whose house in Belfast had been burnt to the ground by Protestant extremists. Their names were Gerry and Doreen. Gerry was long-haired, bearded and nondescript, and wore jeans, training shoes and an imitation leather jacket. Doreen was more fashion-conscious. She owned three pairs of tight, tailored jeans in blue, yellow and white and matching T-shirts and sweaters to go with every pair. She had a mane of curly, red hair which she supplemented with a large pair of tinted glasses that covered half her face.

O'Rafferty was known within the unit as Sarah's husband and Gerry and Doreen continuously cracked jokes about their differences in age. Nothing was said in front of O'Rafferty, however, and he was respected as cell commander, even if he appeared to be rather a bully, who treated his volunteers in the same way as he treated his children.

Sarah was happy being with her uncle, regardless of her insalubrious surroundings, but took a violent, if skilfully concealed, dislike to Doreen who never stopped talking about the nuns in the convent she had been educated in.

When the cell members were not assembling explosive devices, they led normal, working lives. Doreen typed for a Catholic priest who wrote articles in ecclesiastical journals, and Gerry worked as a taxi-driver. Sarah worked as a medical secretary in a London teaching hospital and O'Rafferty spent most of his spare time taking Melissa (comfortably settled in a rented, upmarket, Mayfair flat) to the races.

It was Sarah's career as a medical secretary that would bring about the premature ending of her uncle's life.

Part V

Blenkinsop

It was a mild, sunny day in late September. O'Rafferty had just bought Sarah a Ford Escort van for her birthday. This not only enabled her to go to work, since secretaries were then allowed to leave their cars in hospital car parks. It was also an ideal vehicle for hiding and transporting explosives in.

Sarah felt light-hearted as she entered Doctor's Help Whizkids, an employment agency in Victoria Street, Westminster, which specialized in recruiting temporary, medical secretaries. Copious notices in the window of the agency stated the need for such secretaries in crude, bold letters saying, 'URGENT REPEAT URGENT', followed by a bevy of exclamation marks.

Sarah was wearing a lilac-coloured, leather suit and a leopard-skin scarf. Her hair was arranged in a plait. She walked towards one of three women sitting behind desks and introduced herself.

'What sort of work do you do, Sarah, dear?' asked Caroline James, the woman who ran the agency.

'Copy and audio. No shorthand, I'm afraid. I do purely medical work and am familiar with the terminology. I drive which means I'm flexible about which hospital I work in. I'm prepared to work in both outer and inner London, if required to do so.'

Caroline gave Sarah a beaming smile.

133

'I take it that you've worked in hospitals before?'

Sarah gave the names of two imaginary hospitals in Dublin, the Sacred Heart of Christ our Saviour and the Hospital of St Marguerite. She handed the two references to Caroline, both typed by Seamus on headed paper, using the invented names of two separate doctors.

'As you probably saw from our notices in the window, we are desperately short of temporary, medical secretaries. Most people are so squeamish, they won't go anywhere near a hospital and we are constantly having to turn bookings down. To do this sort of work, we need someone, not only with medical, secretarial skills, but also with a sense of humour,' said Caroline.

Sarah cracked a couple of ribald jokes, neither of them particularly funny. Caroline laughed uproariously and her two colleagues collapsed in hysterical giggles. It crossed Sarah's mind that these women were completely mad.

What typewriters have you used, Sarah?' asked Caroline, when her giggles had subsided.

'All typewriters. I can use manual machines as well as electric. I prefer electric typewriters, though.'

Caroline made Sarah do a typing test. The text she was asked to copy described an operation for open-heart surgery. Sarah handed her work to Caroline.

'I can't say much for your speed, Sarah. It's only forty words a minute. However, your accuracy is absolutely superb. Not one single mistake. That means we can use you.'

Caroline handed Sarah an application form to fill in and as she did so, she studied the CV which Sarah had presented to her on entering the agency.

Caroline had a brief consultation with her two colleagues.

'Take a look at this. Sarah's actually studied Medicine at Trinity College, Dublin, for two years but she had to leave due to injuries in a car accident. She's had experience in every medical faculty, including histopathology.'

Caroline turned to Sarah.

'I can offer you one of many vacancies. Just take your pick; there's X-ray at the Royal Free, ENT at Barts, gynae at the Middlesex, psychiatry at the Westminster, plastic surgery up Harley – Harley Street, that is – and respiratory medicine at Battersea General. What's it to be?'

The long list of names rattled at her made Sarah dizzy. She chose the last post offered.

'Respiratory medicine at Battersea General, please.'

Caroline rang the personnel department at Battersea General.

'I've got just the person you've been screaming for. Her name's Sarah Lloyd. She once studied to be a doctor. She has audio and typing skills and is familiar with all medical terminology.'

'When can you get her here?' asked the personnel officer.

'When can you start, Sarah?' asked Caroline.

'Within the hour, if necessary.'

'She'll be with you within the hour.'

'Excellent!'

'Who do I ask her to report to when she arrives?'

'Tell her to come to Personnel first. Then I'll take her to Dr Blenkinsop, Head of the Department of Respiratory Medicine. She will be working for him.'

Sarah was delighted to have found a job so quickly. She drove to Battersea General and left her van in the hospital car park, using one of the tickets the hospital had issued to her agency. She followed the signs to Personnel.

A tall, handsome woman with red hair and an aquiline profile was standing on the other side of the door as Sarah entered the room. Sarah extended her hand and made a mental decision to return to her original accent.

'I'm Sarah Lloyd from Doctors' Help Whizkids. I understand you require my services in the Department of Respiratory Medicine.'

'We do indeed. We've been waiting for someone to come for two hours already. I expect the agency has told you that you'll be working for the head of the department, Dr Blenkinsop. He's not an easy man to get on with. Three medical secretaries have walked out on him already in the last two weeks. By the way, my name's Enid Shields.'

Sarah was intrigued. She turned to look round the office, which was occupied by four non-medical secretaries working for the personnel managers. Two of the secretaries, one coloured and the other white, were giggling while perusing the application form of a somewhat backward man, who had applied for a job sweeping the paved area outside the hospital.

'Come on, girls,' said Enid, 'you might as well share the joke. Give that to me.'

Against 'Recreations' the man had written: 'Sometimes I sits and thinks; other times I just sits.'

Enid passed the application form to Sarah, covering the applicant's name with her hand for ethical reasons. Sarah giggled.

'All right. Your time's up and the joke's over,' said Enid. 'I'm taking Sarah over to meet Dr Blenkinsop.'

Dr Blenkinsop was not in his office when Enid knocked on his door. The two women walked down the corridor to the front office containing two switchboards. There were two main desks, one of which was occupied by a thirty-year-old housewife called Joan Hopkins. Joan had a long, dour, horse-like face, a pointed nose – the only beautiful feature of her face – and a Cockney accent.

Sarah took one look at this woman and knew instinctively that she would not get on with her. Joan didn't even raise her head to look at Sarah as Enid ushered her to an unoccupied desk.

'Joan,' called Enid.

'Yes. I can't talk for long. I'm very busy.'

'I only want you to meet the new secretary, Sarah Lloyd.'

'Hullo, Sarah.'

'Hullo, Joan,' replied Sarah almost as listlessly.

'I'm hoping that Sarah will stay with us longer than the others,' said Enid.

'Doubt it. Not with Dr Blenkinsop in charge.'

'I wouldn't be too pessimistic. Do you know where he is?'

'Having coffee in the staff room.'

The staff room was the only room in the department where smoking was permitted. It was a pleasant room overlooking a paved area, which was interspersed by the different flowers and shrubs that grow in September. Several uniformed nurses sat on the chairs occupying one side of the room. They were laughing, smoking and joking while pointing at an article in a dog-eared, tabloid newspaper.

On the other side of the room sat three white-coated SHOs* in their early twenties. Among them sat an older man of about fifty. He was not wearing a white coat but an ill-fitting suit which had been handed down to him in his student days.

Sarah ran her eyes over every occupant of the staff room and finally parked them on the fifty-year-old. His bald head was lowered and he was leaning forward in his chair. His skin was pale and seedy-looking and covered with strange, purple patches.

Enid said nothing for the first few moments. Sarah was becoming increasingly impatient. She wanted to get her

---

*SHO: senior house officer. This is a euphemism for a junior doctor.

encounter with Dr Blenkinsop over and done with, so that she could settle down and get on with her work.

'I've waited quite long enough, Enid,' she said, her voice raised in anger. 'Who is this man, Dr Blenkinsop, and where is he now?'

The fifty-year-old man raised his head and looked at Sarah. He had tiny, reddish-green eyes, scarcely larger than a couple of peas, a full, debauched mouth and stale-smelling breath.

'I am Dr Blenkinsop,' he said in a peculiarly breathy voice. 'Aren't you making rather a lot of noise?'

Blenkinsop rose to his feet with difficulty and showed Sarah the way to the front office. He was shorter than she was and as he entered the office, the air was permeated by an unpleasant odour of school kitchens and meat that had gone off. Blenkinsop often had trouble restraining his wind.

Joan taught Sarah how to work the two switchboards and told her what to do. She settled down quickly and worked her way through the tape given to her to type. For the first few days, she remained aloof from the other members of staff. Overtures were made by curious nurses who found Sarah bizarre and mysterious, but Sarah declined all their invitations to lunch because she preferred to eat alone and read the newspapers.

She had been at Battersea General for over a week and still had had no contact with Dr Blenkinsop. His frequent absences from the department inconvenienced his Scottish colleague, Dr Fergus Mackay, an older man who was also a consultant. He was obliged to see all Dr Blenkinsop's patients and in doing so, he often stayed in the clinic until about seven p.m.

Dr Mackay and Dr Blenkinsop were equal in rank and Blenkinsop was head of the department in name only. Both consultants loathed each other and slagged each other off in front of their staff.

The two doctors came from different backgrounds. Dr Mackay was raised in the country a few miles north of Edinburgh. He was the youngest of four children, all boys, and his elder brothers taunted and bullied him by throwing cricket balls at him. His childhood was on the whole somewhat unhappy but he never bore grievances in later life. Although he had a rather fiery temper when inconvenienced, he was a kind-hearted man who liked to laugh and joke with his underlings. He was a socialist but of the Gaitskillian rather than militant school.

Peter George Blenkinsop, known to what few friends he had as Petal Blenkinsop, was an only child, raised single-handedly in a Birmingham slum. He was the son of a prostitute and his unknown father had been one of her clients. His mother's real name was Iris but she was known to her clients as Mademoiselle Wagon-Lit, a name which she chose herself as her son was born prematurely on a train.

Iris was mentally deranged and preferred to call her son Petal. She thought the name was sweet and endearing and would have preferred a daughter to a son so that she could train her to follow her in her trade.

For the first four years of his life, Iris treated Petal like a girl. She made him grow his hair long and every night she forced him to wear curlers. She took him for walks round the backstreets of Birmingham, wearing a starched, white bonnet, a matching dress hemmed with lace, and dancing shoes.

Iris's extreme eccentricity caused Petal Blenkinsop to be the laughing-stock of the Birmingham, backstreet community. She was a doting and indulgent mother who spoiled her son destructively, denying him nothing.

By the time Blenkinsop went to school at the age of five, he had no idea whether he was a boy or a girl and the obligation to wear a grey, flannel suit, instead of a dress and bonnet, confused him even further.

Like the area where he lived, the school which he attended was rough and bullying in the playground was rife. Blenkinsop somehow managed to escape being bullied, and because his effete personality infuriated the boys who actually were bullied, he tended to suck up to the bullies, of whom there were two, both of them twins called Mick and Ned Silver. The twins used Blenkinsop as their spy, a role he doted on. He had no remorse about telling incriminating lies regarding other boys and watching the tough, burly twins rounding up these boys, sitting astride them, grabbing them by the ears and banging their heads on the ground.

Telling lies invariably gave the confused, young Blenkinsop peculiar, sexual pleasure and the more incriminating the lies were, the more he became aroused. He loved to seek the perpetual approval of the Silver twins by filling their Parker pens with ink before lessons and leaving the school during playtime to buy them cigarettes with coins which they provided. Some tobacconists were unwilling to serve Blenkinsop because of his age. He would wait for the shops to become crowded. Then he would steal cigarettes and pocket the money given to him by the twins.

It was a bitterly cold, January day with snow on the ground, the first day of the spring term. Blenkinsop was ten and the Silver twins had just had their fourteenth birthday. Another ten-year-old boy called Ben Lewis had been sent to school with a virus by his mother who wanted him off her hands so that she could go to the cinema. As the master, Mr Henderson, called the register, Lewis was suddenly sick.

'Why did you come to school, Lewis, if you're ill?' asked Henderson.

'Me mam said I had to. She didn't want me at home because she wanted to spend the afternoon at the flicks.'

'That's no excuse, Lewis,' said the master. 'I can't have you starting an epidemic in the school. Will you please tidy up your books and go home.'

'You don't understand, sir. Me mam's locked me out of the house. A man goes in when me dad goes out and that man stays in all morning and gives me mam money to go to the flicks.' A muffled titter went round the class.

Henderson was embarrassed and exasperated. He knew that it was his moral responsibility not to allow a child to become aware of his mother's adultery.

'Have you not got any relatives you can stay with, Lewis?'

'No, sir.'

Blenkinsop had been revelling in the generalized sordidness of this incident and decided to give the master the impression that he was being kind and helpful.

'May I make a suggestion, sir?'

'Yes, Blenkinsop, what is it?'

'It might be a good idea to wait till break. There's a boy in another form who would certainly allow Lewis to rest in his parents' house until Mrs Lewis comes back from the cinema.'

Henderson was becoming bored with the situation.

'All right, all right, Blenkinsop. This boy – is he responsible? That is to say, would he be prepared to take Lewis home during break?'

'Yes, of course he would, sir.'

'Good. That's settled. We have now wasted exactly ten minutes of our valuable time. Will you all please get out your anthologies of the poems of Samuel Taylor Coleridge and turn to page twenty-three. Atkins, stand up and start off by reading the first four verses of *The Rime of the Ancient Mariner*.'

The bell rang for break. Blenkinsop walked over to Lewis who was pale and sweating all over.

'Come on, Ben. I'll soon get you sorted out,' he said

141

kindly. He helped the ailing boy to his feet and took him gently by the arm. 'Put your coat and scarf on. We're going outside.'

Lewis followed him like an automaton. The Silver twins were standing in the corner of the playground. Mick was cleaning his fingernails with a penknife and Ned was smoking a cigarette, facing the wall.

'Hullo, Blenkers,' called Mick. 'Got something for me, have you?'

'Yes. This is Lewis. He came to school with a virus and is spreading it around everywhere. That means the whole school's going to get his germs.'

Lewis was petrified. He had genuinely believed that he was going to be taken to a place to lie down. Ned put out his cigarette and turned round abruptly. The twins advanced menacingly towards Lewis who fell to his hands and knees and was sick on the ground. Blenkinsop stood by laughing.

'Go on, rub his face in it, Ned,' said Mick. And without knowing how dangerous his action would be, Ned obeyed his brother. Lewis choked to death. Blenkinsop rapidly vanished from the scene, no longer wishing to be involved. The twins went off in another direction.

Blenkinsop feigned shock and rushed into the building where he bumped into Henderson, the master.

'What's the news of Lewis, Blenkinsop?'

'Oh, I took him to the locker room and wrapped him up as warmly as I could, and helped him outside to find Power, the nice boy I knew would give him a bed till his mother came home. I looked for Power all over. Then suddenly, Lewis said he felt sick. He ran into the corner of the playground and shouted, "Look the other way, Blenkers!" so I did. I counted to twenty and I found him lying on the ground face downwards. Then I ran to get help and I found you, sir. Can we go over? He's lying so still. I'm terrified he may have died.'

Henderson rushed over to Lewis's body with Blenkinsop hurrying behind him. Henderson turned Lewis over and tried resuscitation which failed. Blenkinsop knelt down by Lewis and forced himself to weep hysterically. Through his bogus tears, he ogled Lewis's pale, motionless face and for the first time in his life, he experienced a strange thrill. It was then that he developed a morbid fascination for death and disease, associated with sexual gratification.

Henderson put his arm round him.

'Are you all right, Blenkinsop?'

'I think so, sir. It's such a shock,' and then he added in a determined tone, almost with reverence, 'I'm going to be a doctor when I grow up.'

'Good lad,' muttered Henderson hoarsely. 'The boy's mother will have to be informed at once. So will the school.' He shuffled down the corridor, mumbling inaudibly.

And the boy, Petal Blenkinsop, did indeed become a doctor in later years but he never grew up.

* * *

Sarah had been working at Battersea General for two weeks. She was a slow but fastidious worker who always checked her work twice before submitting it for signature.

A nurse's voice was heard calling over the tannoy. 'Sarah, will you please go and see Dr Blenkinsop in his office.'

Sarah obeyed. Blenkinsop was sitting behind his desk. He was no longer bald and was wearing a wig which had been intricately interwoven with what little remaining hair he had.

'Your name's Sarah, is it not?' (By now, he had shed his Birmingham accent and had replaced it with an artificial-sounding, upper-class brogue.)

'Yes, that's right, Dr Blenkinsop.'

He bent over and took the duplicated copies of all the work Sarah had done from the top drawer of his desk.

'Is this your work?'

'Yes, Dr Blenkinsop. Is there something wrong with it?'

Blenkinsop gazed into her eyes and smiled lecherously. His teeth were rotten and uneven.

'There's nothing wrong with it at all. In fact, it's absolutely perfect. Not a single mistake. Well done.'

'I'm very glad to hear that, Dr Blenkinsop. Will there be anything further?'

He continued to stare at her. It was a warm day and she was wearing a pale green, leather miniskirt, tan-coloured tights and patent, white, high-heeled boots. She also had on a tight T-shirt with Hieronymus Bosch's *Ship of Fools* printed on it.

'So you like Hieronymus Bosch, do you?' Blenkinsop asked, after a long struggle to find his words.

'Yes, very much so. He's my favourite painter. May I go back and get on with my work now?'

'Your keenness is most impressive and professional,' said the doctor, still baring his rotten teeth. 'Might I ask if you will do me the honour of dining with me tonight?'

'Will you not be dining with your wife?' was all Sarah could think of saying.

'I am divorced. I am in effect inviting you out to dinner.'

Sarah took a look at Blenkinsop and suddenly felt acutely claustrophobic and depressed. She came out in a heavy sweat and she could feel her thick hair sticking to her head.

'I'm so sorry but I'm afraid that won't be possible. I'm living with my partner. We are very much in love and he likes me to be at home every evening.'

Blenkinsop lowered his head and looked offended.

'Your partner, what does he do for a living?'

'Oh, something awfully boring, I'm afraid. He works in the City. He's a stockbroker.'

Blenkinsop continued to stare at Sarah's tanned legs, their colour accentuated by her white boots.

'Are you hoping to marry him?'

'No. Not unless I get pregnant.'

'What type of birth control do you use?'

Sarah shifted from one foot to the other, mortified with embarrassment.

'I've made you blush. How sweet!' said the doctor.

'Dr Blenkinsop, I hope you won't think me rude but these questions are very personal.'

'I can see that I've embarrassed you and I'm sorry, but will you allow me just one more question?'

'Yes. One more only. I've got a lot of work to do.'

'Do you not approve of marriage?'

'Of marriage? No. Not unless there is a pregnancy. You will have to excuse me now. I think you're being rather a naughty boy.'

This aroused Blenkinsop even more. When Sarah wasn't blushing, her smooth, ivory skin reminded him of the dead, of cadavers that had no power to reject his advances.

* * *

The workload in the department was concentrated and strenuous. Next to Sarah's and Joan's office was another office occupied by three more secretaries called Sharon (otherwise known as 'Stinker'), Valerie and Annette. Despite Sarah's lively and humorous overtures, she found no audience in these girls. Valerie and Annette were catty and were jealous of the perks Blenkinsop granted her, such as the freedom to go to the cinema every Friday afternoon, which she covered herself for by saying that she was having physiotherapy for an allegedly bad back.

The woman Sarah disliked most of all was Stinker. Stinker was offensively genteel. She had a gratingly high-pitched voice and spoke like a schoolgirl, with a pronounced lisp. Apart from that, she had an irritating habit of sniffing all the time.

145

Often, on entering the office, she would state primly, 'There'th one word I don't ever wish to hear uttered in thith offith and that'th a word whith beginth with an F.'

Sarah heard her and bombarded her with foul language. Stinker later made the foolish mistake of criticizing the controversial Sir Jasper Montrose, Sarah's God. In retaliation, Sarah rubbed out one of Stinker's tapes and also removed an urgent message taken by Stinker, and left on Dr Mackay's desk.

There was a changing room and a shower in the department which Sarah always used at the end of the day, to enable her to be clean, perfumed and groomed for O'Rafferty, as there were no bathing facilities in their lodgings. On the outer wall of the shower-room, was a reproduced etching of the hospital as it was a hundred years ago. Behind the picture was a small hole, drilled by Blenkinsop so that he could watch the ablutions of any woman who took his fancy.

Sarah had no idea that she was being watched. She undressed slowly and neatly folded up all her clothes which she put in a tidy pile on a chair. She turned on the shower and sprayed herself with a gush of cold water which made her jump into the air like a cat, wrapping her arms round her chest.

Blenkinsop peered through the hole and felt sick with unrequited lust. As Sarah lathered herself all over with a cake of honey-scented soap, he began to touch himself. This only increased his torment. He tore off his stethoscope and white coat, which covered his ill-fitting, dark grey suit, nervously tweaked the knot in his tie and strode purposefully towards the mortuary.

*   *   *

In the Whitechapel flat, Doreen was cooking bacon and eggs, sausages and fried bread. There were a few

146

cans of beer on the unset kitchen table which was covered with brimming ashtrays and un-wiped up messes from previous meals. O'Rafferty was sitting in the kitchen, smoking a pipe, surveying the slovenly room with mounting irritation.

'Doreen, for Christ's sake get this table cleaned up!'

'Can't you see I'm cooking, Seamus?'

'All right, all right. Have you seen Sarah yet?'

'No, she's not come in.'

'And Gerry?'

'He's sleeping. He didn't sleep too well last night.'

'I don't care whether he slept well last night or not. Get him up and have him clean up in here.'

'OK, Seamus.'

Gerry came in, wearing a dirty, pale grey track suit which he had worn day and night for over a week. He looked bleary-eyed and a smouldering cigarette burned from the corner of his mouth.

'Get the kitchen cleaned, Gerry,' said O'Rafferty. 'You're not over here to sleep all day.'

Gerry did not stand up to O'Rafferty. He went to the sink where dirty plates had accumulated, filled the sink with cold water (there was no hot water), poured cleansing liquid over the plates and washed and rinsed them. Then he cleaned and laid the table.

Sarah came in about half an hour later and found O'Rafferty in their room.

'I thought something had happened to you, lassie. You're not normally this late.'

'I had some work to catch up on for Petal Blenkinsop.'

'Petal Blenkinsop! Petal bloody Blenkinsop! What kind of person would have a name like that? What's he like, Sarah?' asked O'Rafferty.

Sarah went over to her uncle and sat on his knee.

'He's a dirty, old man and he's so hideous to look at

that I can't even look him in the face when I speak to him. I saw him pawing a nurse's tits yesterday.'

O'Rafferty hugged his niece and kissed her on the cheek.

'But he's *hideous*, Uncle Seamus. He looks like a weather-beaten, old bulldog. He wears a wig which is often askew, particularly when he runs across the square in the wind. He says my work's very good though, and the other people there aren't too bad.'

O'Rafferty suddenly turned Sarah over and slapped her bottom.

'What was that for?'

'You're sliding back into that Brit accent again. Watch it!'

The four cell members sat down at the kitchen table and helped themselves to the food which sizzled in the frying pan in the centre. They filled their glasses with beer and drank.

O'Rafferty was the first to break the silence.

'We've got a major job to do this Saturday,' he said, draining his glass. 'We've orders to do in Sir Geoffrey Harcourt-Webster. We've already checked the layout of his house and grounds.'

'Who the hell's he?' asked Sarah.

'Oh, come on now, Sare. He's the bloody Secretary of State for Northern Ireland. He's a bachelor and when he's off duty, he's a recluse. He lives in a big Tudor place three and a half miles north of Poynings in Sussex. He has a cleaner in in the mornings but for the rest of the day he fends for himself.'

The beer was releasing Sarah's inhibitions but she still managed to affect her Irish accent.

'That reminds me of something that happened to me in Wimbledon once. I was propositioned in the street by this weird dwarf who was known for some reason as "Lackie",' she said.

Gerry and Doreen laughed.

'So Lackie said to me: "Would you like to come home for a coffee? I've got this Tudor place up the road." I should have known that there are no Tudor houses in Wimbledon. So what did Lackie do? He took me up three flights of stairs to a bedsit and all I saw was a black and white striped wall!'

'Come on now, Sarah!' said O'Rafferty. 'Why can't you keep to the matter in hand? We're going to the house at three o'clock on Saturday afternoon. Gerry, you will do the job and ride in front with Sarah who'll be driving the van. I'll be in the back with Doreen.'

Sarah felt sleepy on Saturday afternoon so she drank two cups of black coffee, to enable her to drive the powerful van which O'Rafferty had given her. It no longer alarmed her that she had lost her conscience. The idea of participating in the murder of a man she didn't even hate, seemed of no more significance to her than an adventure and an opportunity to please her uncle.

She could never forget the injustice of her brother, Selwyn, being taken from her. She remembered how he had emigrated to Australia with his tall, Australian wife and had set up a lucrative business there.

At the end of Selwyn's stay in London, of one week's duration, Sarah had driven him and his wife to the airport. She had watched from the balcony in the departure lounge as they boarded the plane. She had even watched it take off and disappear through the thick, black clouds. She had no idea when she would see Selwyn again, if ever. She had returned to her parents' house and had gone to bed early. She had felt as if she had witnessed her brother's execution and remembered how the icy, grey jumbo jet had roared like a bomb into the sky.

As she had wept silently into her pillow, she had clawed at the sheets, having reached the conclusion that no

Supreme Being could possibly exist if such chronic unhappiness was being forced on her, when she herself had done no wrong. She remembered her school days. Although she had loved her school, she had resented having to attend spiritual instruction classes and hearing the teaching that virtue begats reward. Had she not been virtuous all her early life? Why should her beloved brother have been taken away to another continent? The phrase, 'Ask and thou wilt receive' had provoked a rage reaction within her.

How many times had she said: 'Please bring Selwyn home?' How many times had her plea been unanswered?

It was then that the men in white coats had been called out and after a few weeks, the world-powerful businessman, publisher and newspaper proprietor, Sir Jasper Montrose, a friend of her other brother, Mivart, had carried Sarah from the mental institution in which she had been incarcerated, like a babe in arms and had nursed her back to health.

Sir Jasper Montrose was an extremely large, handsome man, who was regarded by some as a 'crook' where his financial dealings were concerned. Sarah worshipped him on account of his good looks as well as his charismatic, rough-diamond kindness. He had become her new Supreme Being and even after he suffered death by drowning, she would kneel and pray to him before the photographs of him in her bedroom, of which there were thirty-two.

The two sad events in her life had made Sarah callous. The idea of killing was a sexual stimulant to her. Her sadistic streak prompted her to make others suffer although she couldn't have cared less whether Britain got out of Ulster or not.

'Come on, Sare. Keep that speed down. You're day-dreaming. You're supposed to keep within the limits,' exclaimed O'Rafferty, interrupting Sarah's sad memories.

They were on the London to Brighton dual carriageway, which was surprisingly uncrowded for a Saturday afternoon.

'OK, Seamus.' She decreased her speed to forty m.p.h.

'Good on you, lassie! That's more like it.'

Sir Geoffrey Harcourt-Webster, the Secretary of State for Northern Ireland, was in his swimming pool at the time that he was to be delivered into the Reaper's clutches. The IRA had had him under long-term surveillance. He was a man who favoured complete solitude and was floating on his back, letting the warm, afternoon sun tan his face.

'Go slowly up the drive and turn round, ready to get out,' commanded O'Rafferty.

Gerry had loaded his firearm which had a silencer on it. He went up to the house and rang the bell. For over five minutes, no one answered, although Harcourt-Webster's Bentley was parked just outside the front door and a fat, golden Labrador slept peacefully in the driveway. Gerry went over to O'Rafferty, who was sitting in the back of the van.

'There's no one there. Just the car.'

'Don't be daft!' rasped O'Rafferty. 'Search the garden.'

It didn't take long for Gerry to find his victim who was floating, his eyes closed, enjoying the warm, autumn sun, suspecting nothing.

Gerry moved slowly towards the edge of the swimming pool. He pointed his gun at Harcourt-Webster's head and fired.

The bullet only grazed his forehead. The Secretary of State screamed and flapped his arms and legs around in the water.

Gerry fired two more shots. One hit his victim in the stomach, the other in the chest. There was a groaning, gurgling noise just before Harcourt-Webster's body became submerged, the water one massive lake of blood.

Gerry rushed back to the van, its engine still running and scrambled in.

'Go like fuck, Sare!' yelled O'Rafferty.

Sarah obeyed, her speed climbing to thirty m.p.h. within one minute; she was screeching the brakes and churning up the gravel. Suddenly, she realized that she had driven over something. She looked in the mirror and saw the Secretary of State's soporific Labrador crushed beyond hope of survival.

She thumped the steering wheel in despair.

'Oh, my God, I've killed a dog! I saw it as I drove up to the front door. It was a beautiful, golden Labrador.'

She drove erratically down the sinuous drive, flanked by rhododendrons. She began to sob and scream hysterically. O'Rafferty tried to comfort her by massaging her shoulders.

'Go on driving till we get off the premises. Then pull into the side and get out of the van, calmly and slowly. Doreen, don't just sit there like an idle, suet pudding! Get your ass in the driver's seat and snap it up!' he shouted.

He opened the back door for Sarah to get in beside him.

'It's all right, lassie. There are other dogs like that about. Try to imagine how heartbroken the dog would have been on finding out that its master had been killed, eh?'

The comforting words calmed Sarah, so typically English in her sentimentality about animals, if not about humans. She sat staring vacantly into space.

There was a long traffic jam on the way into London. Gerry smiled slyly, waited for three-quarters of an hour and turned on the radio. First, there were a few loud, jingling advertisements with O'Rafferty's booming voice drowning the noise.

'For Christ's sake turn that bloody thing down!'

Gerry decreased the volume. Then, the news announcer's solemn voice was heard.

'Here is an announcement. Sir Geoffrey Harcourt-Webster, Secretary of State for Northern Ireland, was shot dead in the swimming pool at his country home in Sussex earlier this afternoon. His pet dog was run over by the getaway car. It is thought that the IRA is responsible for his murder. Apparently, there were no witnesses.'

O'Rafferty grabbed hold of the car radio and shouted into it: 'The IRA is responsible for the killing of Sir Geoffrey Harcourt-Webster and the code word is "Bastards".'

* * *

Sarah arrived at Battersea General fifteen minutes late on Monday morning. She had on her thigh-high, white boots, a red leather miniskirt and a red and white striped T-shirt. Dr Blenkinsop had his back to her as she entered the office. He was addressing a petite West Indian woman with a hearing deficiency. She was a filing clerk and Blenkinsop treated her like a village idiot. His tone when addressing her was sarcastic and he pronounced each word he uttered with clipped precision.

'Of late, patients have had difficulty locating – oh, sorry finding – the doctors' office. You will please ensure – oh, sorry, I meant see – that a large notice is put on the wall in the corridor saying DOCTORS' OFFICE in capital letters, followed by an arrow pointing to the doctors' office. That is to say – an arrow showing where the doctors' office is.'

The clerk was so mesmerized by Blenkinsop's mode of speech that she looked at him aghast.

'Do we have a problem, dear?'

'No. I understand you, Dr Blenkinsop.'

'Good. So perhaps you could get on with the matter in hand. Just print the words with a black, felt-tip pen.

Incidentally, you do know how to spell "doctor" don't you?'

'Yes, thank you, Dr Blenkinsop.'

'I'm *so* glad. I thought perhaps you might be having a problem.'

Sarah overheard the conversation and concluded that Blenkinsop was a brick short of a load. When he saw her through the corner of his eye, he turned round hurriedly, facing her. She had not slept at all for the past two nights, because she had been so traumatized by the death of the Secretary of State's dog. She turned round to face Blenkinsop.

His recognition of her upper-class accent endeared his provincially snobbish attitude towards her. His demeanour changed abruptly from Hyde to Jekyll, while the dumbfounded clerk looked for a felt-tip pen before putting up the notice.

'Hullo, Sarah, love. Don't you look sexy!'

Blenkinsop's personal appearance was so repellent that Sarah couldn't look him in the eye. She stared at the floor, thinking that she would be happier to be ogled by the Elephant Man even, rather than by the thing standing in front of her.

'Your eyes are red from weeping, love.' (He frequently addressed women he fancied as 'love', due to his proverbial commonness.) 'What is it, love? Has someone upset you?'

The memory of the crushed, golden Labrador surged through Sarah's mind. She burst into tears. Blenkinsop put his arm round her. The tight, white coat he had on stank of formaldehyde.

'Come on, love. I'll make you a cup of coffee. Then we can have a chat in private.'

Sarah and Blenkinsop sat on the same side of a desk covered with papers. She crossed her artificially tanned legs for her own comfort rather than for flaunting purposes.

Blenkinsop laid his hand on her thigh but she swiftly pulled back her chair.

'Come on. Tell me. A trouble shared is a trouble halved.'

'It's nothing serious,' said Sarah. 'I received a very hostile letter from my bank manager this morning, claiming that I was two hundred pounds overdrawn, and he asked me to surrender my cheque book to the bank.'

Blenkinsop was puzzled. Sarah's accent had led him to assume that she was from a wealthy family. It crossed his mind that her parents may have forced her to fend for herself and learn to be independent.

'I think I might be able to help you,' he said, smiling. 'Since I'm the head of the department, I'd like – that is with your permission – to take you on as a permanent member of staff. Technically speaking, you would start as a higher clerical officer which does not carry too large a salary. However, I do a lot of private reports every week and I pay fifteen pounds in cash for each one. In the meantime, perhaps I could advance you a loan of the two hundred pounds that you owe the bank to save you from your present embarrassment.'

Sarah managed to look Blenkinsop in the eye for a fleeting moment. She knew that it was in her interests to accept his offer, even if it meant resigning when O'Rafferty was called back to Ireland.

'Well?' said Blenkinsop. 'What do you think of my offer, or would you like a few days to think about it?'

Sarah uncrossed her legs and leant forward in her chair.

'I am truly indebted to you, Dr Blenkinsop. It would be an honour to accept your offer,' she said enthusiastically.

'Oh, bless you, love! I know how well you and I are going to get on. I will confirm with Personnel and you can fill in the paperwork. Then I will announce the good news at our next departmental meeting in two days' time.

Joan, with whom Sarah shared an office, had heard rumours that this was going to happen.

'Morning, Joan,' said Sarah amicably.

Joan heard but refused to answer. She envied Sarah's extreme beauty and self-confidence which bordered on arrogance.

'I said "good morning, Joan",' Sarah repeated.

Joan looked up from her papers.

'Is it true you're going permanent?' she asked, her voice flat and surly.

'If you want to know what goes on here, you should ask Dr Blenkinsop or Dr Mackay.'

'I've 'eard it said that Dr Blenkinsop does you special favours because 'e fancies you. You don't deserve rank because you work so slowly. 'E does fancy you, doesn't 'e?'

Sarah fed a sheet of paper and two carbons into her typewriter.

'What man wouldn't?' she answered.

* * *

The four cell members were sitting down to their evening meal, eating a Chinese takeaway which had been heated up by Doreen.

Friction had gradually built up between Doreen and Sarah. Doreen was irritated by Sarah's sentimental reaction to the death of the Secretary of State's dog and by Gerry's apparent sympathy for Sarah.

Gerry said, 'I can fully understand why Sarah was upset when she killed that dog. When I was about ten, I had a pet collie which was run over by a pig-sixer* just outside our door in the Falls Road. I think it was that that first drew me to militant republicanism.'

---

*Pig-sixer – IRA slang for an armoured truck.

Doreen pushed the beansprouts round her plate with her fork in her right hand, rested her left elbow on the table and ran her hand through her mane of uncombed, red hair.

'For Christ's sake, Gerry! Why do you have to sympathise with Sarah? She never helps with the meals or the washing up or anything. I have to do it all myself.'

O'Rafferty had been struggling to keep his temper. He banged his fist on the table.

'Doreen, would you stop having a go at Sarah! She works for far longer hours than you and has to travel further to get to and from work.'

'So?'

'What the hell do you mean, "So"? Every morning, she has to drive all the way over to Battersea where she works a seven and a half hour day in the hospital. Then she drives back in heavy traffic. She's exhausted by the end of the day. All you have to do is walk a few yards down the road to do your typing for that man.'

Doreen was afraid to stand up to O'Rafferty. She looked at Sarah in an attempt to catch her eye and give her a reproachful look, but Sarah was bending over her plate, busy shovelling food into her mouth. Doreen turned to Gerry.

'Gerry, don't you think this is unfair? Why should I have to do everything myself?'

'Sure, it's not unfair,' said Gerry. 'You heard what Seamus said. You've got the easiest job of the four of us, so it's up to you to do all the domestic work. Apart from that, this place is filthy. It's time you cleaned it up.'

Doreen didn't take kindly to the universal opinion of her comrades. After giving Sarah an eye-piercing glare, she lowered her head and pushed her plate aside.

'OK, Gerry, Seamus, Sarah,' she muttered.

* * *

The following evening, Sarah was late coming back so the preparation of dinner had to be delayed. Blenkinsop had asked her to stay on, to type a private patient's report. When she returned, there was an eerie atmosphere in the room. The pregnant silence was broken by O'Rafferty.

'How would you like to go out and do a job yourself, Sarah? It would give you a bit more self-confidence,' he said.

Sarah pushed her hair back from her face. 'What do you want me to do, Seamus?'

'On your way to work tomorrow, we want you to leave this plastic bag outside the police station near the hospital.' He pointed at a white, plastic bag, precariously balanced against the wall in a corner of the room. 'You're to leave it there at eight o'clock. The bomb is to go off at eight fifty-five. I can guarantee that there won't be any dogs involved.'

Sarah felt honoured to have gained so much of O'Rafferty's trust that he was prepared to set her a task such as this.

'I'll need someone to drive the van, in case I have to make a quick getaway,' she said.

O'Rafferty turned to Doreen. 'After Sarah leaves the bag, you will drive her to her hospital. Sarah, you will wear your red wig and dark glasses while you're leaving the bag. Once the van is a fair distance from the police station, you will take them off and push them under the seat.'

'Yes. I'll do that, Seamus.'

'What about you, Doreen? Are your instructions clear?'

Doreen looked at Sarah, envious of her beauty and her popularity with the two men in the cell.

'Clear as an unmuddied lake, Seamus. Clear as an azure sky in deepest summer.'

That night, Sarah knelt down on the lavatory floor and pulled out the locket from round her neck, in which lay a photograph of Sir Jasper Montrose. She wrenched it open like a mussel and held it close to her face.

'O, Jas, who hailest from the Carpathian Mountains and who art born half Cossack and half bear, help me to please my uncle in every way and help me to carry out his orders in the interests of what is most dear to him. Above all else, help me to conceive his child.'

She kissed the photograph in the locket and clipped it shut. Then she placed it round her neck. She went into the bedroom, lay down beside O'Rafferty and allowed her adoration for him to take its physical course.

Doreen was sitting behind the wheel of the Ford Escort van, impatiently revving up the engine, with half her face covered by a black scarf like Dick Turpin. Sarah came out of the building carrying the bag, wearing a pale green, leather suit, training shoes, a red wig with a fringe and tinted, green glasses. She left the bag in the back of the van, got into the passenger seat slowly and put on her seatbelt without speaking to Doreen.

'Are you walking in your sleep, Sarah?'

Sarah had had about as much of Doreen as she could take. She lit a cigarette. After she had inhaled, she decided to let her comrade know that she would tolerate her behaviour no longer. She spoke in a strange, deep voice, only just managing to retain her Irish accent.

'Engage gear. Head for Battersea. Step on it!'

Neither spoke for the next few moments. When they reached the police station, Doreen pulled into the side of the road and stopped. The time was eight o'clock. The two women sat in silence for five minutes. Sarah undid her seatbelt and opened the passenger's door, carrying the bag.

'Wait here. Keep the engine running. I suspect you have it in mind to drive off and leave me here. I advise you not to. Seamus O'Rafferty is the most formidable kneecapper in the IRA. Get it?'

159

Doreen caught Sarah's eye and bared her yellow teeth in a snarling grimace. Sarah inadvertently inhaled a whiff of Doreen's stale breath and started retching.

'Getting cold feet are you, Shamie's moll?'

'No. I just wish you'd clean your bloody teeth occasionally.'

Sarah wasn't nervous then or even guilty about the loss of life that her action would cause, but her hatred for Doreen was so vehement that her hands began to shake and she started to hyperventilate. She placed the bag in a dustbin outside the police station, walked back to the van and got in.

Doreen pulled away and tuned into Radio London.

'Do we have to listen to pop music at this hour of the day?' said Sarah as she removed her wig and glasses before putting them under her seat.

'I like it,' said Doreen.

'That means you must have an IQ of minus a hundred and twenty.'

Doreen turned the volume up. Sarah snapped the radio off and pushed in a cassette of *The Marriage of Figaro*.

'Ever heard of a fella called Mozart?' she barked.

'No. Has precious Shamie boy told you that he's our next target?'

Sarah could take no more of this ignorant, foul-breathed woman. She gave her a resounding slap on the ear. Then she wound down her window and put her head out of it as if she were about to be sick.

'Why are you leaning out of the window, attracting attention?' asked Doreen.

'Because your breath stinks like a decomposing corpse.'

They arrived at the hospital car park.

'Get out of the van and give me the keys,' said Sarah.

As they both got out, Doreen hurled the keys at Sarah. It was eight-thirty. Blenkinsop happened to be walking across the car park. Sarah bent over to pick up the keys. She turned round abruptly as Doreen crept up behind her.

'What are you doing, Doreen? You're supposed to be going to work.'

Doreen was considerably less articulate than Sarah and stared straight through her, her eyes seething with venom. By this time, Blenkinsop was five yards away from them. Doreen summed up her loathing for her comrade in a few screaming words: 'Tart! Whore! Slag!'

'Hullo, Sarah,' said Blenkinsop. 'Who is that woman? Is there some kind of problem?'

'Oh, she told me that she was a psychiatric patient. She came up to me as I was locking up my van and asked me where the nearest sex shop was. She got annoyed because I said I didn't know.'

By this time, Doreen had disappeared. Blenkinsop started giggling.

'Poor, old Sarah! Come on in and we'll have some coffee together before we clear my desk. As you know, we've got the cardiac catheterization meeting this morning. Joan's taking the minutes, so after we've cleared my desk, you'll have to man the two switchboards and operate the tannoy. Sorry to have made you and everyone else come in half an hour early. This is an important day.'

'That's all right, Dr Blenkinsop. I don't mind manning the switchboards. It will make a change,' said Sarah.

Blenkinsop screwed his hideous face into an even more hideous smile.

'Oh, bless you, love!' he said in a tone that was almost Monrovian in its breathiness.

An agency temp had been assigned to clear up the filing overload that week. Her job was to put all the electrocardiogram results in alphabetical order, photocopy each one and clip the originals to the front of the patients' casenotes. She was a Cockney and her name was Tracey Swift.

Sarah didn't recognize her when she saw her in the

front office. She felt annoyed because she wanted the room to herself so that she could put her feet up and smoke while handling the switchboards.

The two women introduced themselves. Then Tracey got on with her duties while Sarah sat on a swivel chair with her feet on the desk and read *Crime and Punishment*. The book fascinated her but also had a disturbing effect on her. She lit a cigarette and continued reading.

'You do know that you're not allowed to smoke in the front office, don't you?' said Tracey.

When reading any book, describing a murderer's heavy, emotional conflict and, as in this instance, this particular book, Sarah felt despondent and her behaviour became hostile and pompous.

'I would remind you that you are only an agency temp, whereas I enjoy the rank of higher clerical officer. You will kindly not issue orders to me and you will show sufficient respect for my rank by addressing me as "Officer".'

Tracey had not been graced with great intelligence. She was intimidated by Sarah who talked like a bad-tempered, old colonel.

'Sorry, Officer,' said the timid temp. 'I will remember to address you as "Officer" in future.'

As Tracey got on with her work and Sarah waited for calls to come in, a sudden explosion was heard. It was so violent that even the walls of the building shook.

Tracey started screaming and threw herself under a desk while Sarah continued reading.

'I'm sorry, Officer!' Tracey bleated, 'I've always been scared stiff of thunder.'

Sarah lit another cigarette.

'There's no need to be afraid of thunder. Get out from under there and do your work.'

Within a few minutes, calls came in in droves. Many of them were for the casualty department, but incompetent switchboard operators had routed them through to the Department of Respiratory Medicine.

Sarah became increasingly irritated. When the next call came in, she put the second caller on hold.

'Respiratory medicine,' she said.

A furious male voice, showing a regional accent, boomed down the line like a battering ram. Sarah had to hold the receiver a yard away from her ear.

'This is Crumblebottom and Bongwit, funeral directors!' yelled the man. 'A navy blue, Polish Lada, registration number FBL 705K, has been parked outside the mortuary. We can't get our blooming 'earses in to pick up the stiffs, blast it!'

'Do you use this kind of language when you speak to the bereaved?' asked Sarah.

'Don't get uppity with me, lady!' barked the man. 'There's been a massive IRA bomb. The whole place is awash with stiffs.'

Sarah felt a slight jolt. She was unaware that a mere carrier bag could cause so much carnage. A twinge of guilt passed through her but it was short-lived.

'Hullo! Hullo! Hullo!' shouted the man from Crumblebottom and Bongwit.

'Do stop shouting "hullo". I have to hold the receiver a yard away from my ear whenever you speak,' said Sarah. 'The car could belong to anyone. What the hell do you expect me to do about it?'

The man went on shouting. Sarah hung up. She put the other line on hold and lit another cigarette.

'Respiratory medicine.'

This time, a man with a more cultured accent was on the line but he, too, was shouting at the top of his voice.

'Kenyon's Funeral Directors here. A navy blue, Polish Lada, registration number FBL 705K is blocking the mortuary gates. Can you get it moved?'

'Why the hell do you all have to ring me up about this car? Why can't you call Security?'

'We already have. They've told us that the car is owned by someone in your department.'

'Hold on, please.'

The other phone was ringing at the same time. Each caller was in some way connected with the funeral business. While Tracey was filing, Sarah developed a bad headache and was getting thoroughly fed up.

'Come on, Tracey! This is an emergency. You've got to help me with the switchboards. I can't handle all the calls on my own.'

'I was told only to do the filing, Officer.'

Sarah grabbed Tracey by the arm and dragged her across the room.

'I'm not interested in what you were told to do! Help me with the phones or I'll have you thrown out.'

The situation was completely out of control. The telephones were all ringing at once and the room sounded like an American newspaper proprietor's office on the eve of an execution.

Sarah grabbed hold of the tannoy. Blenkinsop, Mackay, the senior registrar, senior house officers, clinical assistants and senior nurses were sitting in an office used as a boardroom, reviewing the progress of each respiratory patient, ignorant of the commotion in the front office.

A rasping, deep voice caused all these people to jump, as the tannoy boomed through the entire department, including the ward reserved for the terminally ill, where a priest knelt by the side of a gasping man in a curtained bed and prayed.

'A navy blue, Polish Lada, registration number FBL 705K, has been parked outside the mortuary,' Sarah's colonel's voice stated grimly. 'Will the owner of this vehicle

164

please remove it without delay. I have had substantial complaints from more than five different funeral directors.' She paused and added, her voice an octave lower, 'The hearses are unable to gain access to the building to pick up the bodies.'

Two junior nurses on the ward giggled nervously.

'That's Dr Blenkinsop's car! Dr Mackay isn't going to like this one bit, is he?' said one of them.

In the boardroom, Mackay scowled across the table at Blenkinsop whose head was bowed in embarrassment. The senior house officers tittered helplessly into their hands. Blenkinsop rose slowly from his chair and shuffled out of the room. He went straight to the front office. Sarah had just managed to put her cigarette out as he entered the room.

'Was that your voice on the tannoy, Sarah? You sounded like the bloody Gestapo!' shouted Blenkinsop.

'Does that car outside the mortuary belong to you, Dr Blenkinsop?'

'That's none of your business.'

'It most certainly is my business. I've had foul-mouthed funeral directors raining in on me on all these lines for the whole morning.'

Blenkinsop was attracted by Sarah's defiance as well as her beauty. He turned his head away and blushed. Then he walked over to her and put his hand on her shoulder.

'Here are the keys. Do me a favour and move it for me, love. Shove it somewhere in the car park.'

'Can you not move it yourself?'

'Well, you know how it is. An irate hearse driver would hit a man but he wouldn't be likely to strike a woman.'

'All right. I'll do it but next time please use the car park. I don't want a repetition of what I had to go through on your account.'

Blenkinsop smiled.

'Tomorrow morning at nine-thirty, you and I will have a little chat in my office,' he said.

'All right. Nothing bad I hope.'

'Oh, no, just a friendly little chat.'

* * *

Sarah was excited at the end of the day by the opportunity she would have of telling O'Rafferty about her adventure. As she drove to Whitechapel, the words on a newspaper placard hit her across the face like a wet towel: 'IRA BOMB KILLS 48'.

She pulled in to buy a copy of the *Evening Standard*. Across the front page splashed the words, 'A bomb exploded outside Battersea Police Station at eight fifty-five this morning, killing forty-eight people. A mother and her two small children were killed instantly. No warning was given. The IRA has said it was responsible for the incident. The police are looking for two women with red hair.'

A feeling of dismay suddenly descended on Sarah. She drove on and found a pub. She pulled up outside it, went in and ordered two double gin and tonics before returning to Whitechapel.

O'Rafferty was standing on the doorstep with his arms outstretched as if welcoming a child home from school.

'I'm proud of you, lassie!' he said. 'But we didn't mean to cause so much civvie cazh. I hope it didn't upset you.'

'Well, it did before I knocked back two double gins. Have a look at the paper. Two small children were killed.'

'Would you have got soppy about German children dying in the Second World War?' asked O'Rafferty.

'No, but this has upset me a bit. Quite apart from that, I don't ever want to see that bitch Doreen again. After she dropped me at the hospital, she shouted in public that I was a tart, a whore and a slag. I can't cope with her, Uncle Seamus.'

O'Rafferty sat down on a poorly-lined chair in the hall and took Sarah on his knee.

'We'll get rid of her, Sare. No one in the world speaks to my lassie like that.'

'How?'

'Doreen will meet with an accident. We'll shoot her and make it look like suicide.'

'When?'

'When I say. That's when.'

* * *

At nine-thirty the following morning, Sarah knocked on the door of Blenkinsop's office. The doctor was sitting behind his desk with his briefcase open, sucking a foul-smelling, Havana cigar.

'Sit down, Sarah, love. How was your journey to work?'

'All right. Why?'

Blenkinsop pulled his chair back from his desk. It was evident that his words were not coming easily to him.

'Sarah,' he began, 'I feel that only I can say a thing like this to you because I am closest to you in this department.'

He paused and relit his cigar which had gone out.

'Sarah, the truth of the matter is – we're all desperately worried about the sound of your voice over the tannoy system. It really is having a terrifying effect on the nurses, not to mention my terminally ill patients. Why, for instance, did you have to mention the word "hearses" during one of your earth-shattering pronouncements?'

'Hearses exist, Dr Blenkinsop, and there are times when they have to be mentioned, particularly on occasions when your car is preventing them from getting to the mortuary. Would you prefer it if I called them "slow blacks" instead?'

Blenkinsop drank the rest of his coffee, which was cold,

and, in a gesture of Victorian, northern gentility, he dabbed his lips with his handkerchief.

'What you could have done,' he said delicately, because he was afraid of Sarah, 'would have been to give the number of the car and ask its owner to move it because it was in the way, instead of going into details that would upset my patients. One of them, in fact, was receiving the last rites from a gentleman of the cloth and on hearing your voice, he was so terrified that he expired. Apparently, his blood spurted all over the priest's clothing when he rattled.'

Sarah couldn't control herself any longer. She had manic, hysterical giggles which she tried to disguise with a fit of coughing.

Suddenly, Blenkinsop, too, got the giggles.

'Go along, Sarah, love. I could do with another cup of coffee,' he said.

* * *

When Sarah got back to Whitechapel that evening, she met a young woman called Helen who was sitting drinking beer with O'Rafferty and Gerry. O'Rafferty introduced Helen to Sarah who took an instinctive liking to her. She had long, fair hair and was shy and quiet, but beneath her gentle exterior there lurked a spirit of determined and uncompromising republicanism.

'Helen's my new girlfriend,' said Gerry, holding Helen round the waist.

'What's happened to Doreen?' Sarah asked casually.

'You won't ever be seeing her again,' said O'Rafferty, in a brutal tone.

'Is she dead, then?'

'I've just said that you won't ever be seeing her again and that's the end of it.'

'Seamus?'

'Yes, what is it?'

'I've got something very important to tell you.'

'What, lassie?'

'I'm having a baby. I found out this afternoon, at the hospital.'

O'Rafferty put his arms round his niece and kissed her.

'Oh, my darling, little lassie!' he said, this time talking to himself, 'It doesn't matter at all if you kill, as long as you bring someone into the world.'

There was an addition to the short-staffed workforce in the Department of Respiratory Medicine. Sarah had been sent to Personnel to pick the newcomer up.

'Where's our new girl?' she asked, once in the offices of Personnel.

One of the girls pointed to a middle-aged woman, her face framed by a shock of cascading, golden curls. She sat in a huddled heap, looking as if all her relatives had been run over by a bus.

'Sarah, this is Hilda Saunderson. Sarah's going to take you over to the Department of Respiratory Medicine,' said the Personnel girl.

Sarah introduced herself to Hilda.

'You will be working in the same department as me,' she said in an authoritarian voice. 'You'll be replacing Stinker whom I sent packing on Friday,' and added, 'Stinker and I had had a blockbuster.'

Hilda observed Sarah's face with a look of curiosity but friendliness. Hilda had an unusual voice, its brogue completely unattributed to region or class. She was about forty years old. When she spoke, Sarah felt no discomfort but an unexplained eeriness which fascinated her. Hilda's eyes were of a Caribbean blue. She fixed them on Sarah's.

'I've seen you before,' said Hilda in an uncanny tone, 'but in another life. You used to rob graves.'

169

'I beg your pardon?'

'I know we've met before, hundreds of years ago.'

'That's as may be,' said Sarah, 'and now we're meeting again. You're damned odd but there's something about you that I know I'm going to like.'

During the course of the next few weeks, Sarah and Hilda became inseparable friends. Hilda told Sarah everything about her family and her life at home. Sarah could tell Hilda nothing but listened fascinated to what Hilda told her.

Hilda's husband was very clumsy about the house and had a violent and uncontrollable temper. He was known to her as 'Napoleon' because of his facial resemblance to the Emperor. Inadvertently, he repeatedly dropped crockery onto the floor and felt so frustrated and angry with himself, that he would bang his head against a wall for minutes at a time, with such alarming ferocity that he sounded like someone demolishing a building.

'He sounds like a character out of a slapstick comedy,' said Sarah. 'If you don't give him an audience, he'll soon stop banging his head against the wall.'

The two women were in a pub near the hospital, drinking vodka and tonic so that they wouldn't smell of alcohol when they returned to the office.

'Why don't you ever say anything about your partner, Sarah?' asked Hilda.

'There's not much to say. He's unemployed but he's wealthy because his parents left him a big inheritance. He's got a flat in Victoria.'

'But you said he lived in Whitechapel.'

'Oh, he did live in Whitechapel. Well, just to be close to the London Hospital in Whitechapel Road. He used to attend the migraine clinic there but now he's much better. He hates the area and he's moved.'

Lies had always come more easily than the truth to

170

Sarah, so much so, that she no longer knew the difference between truth and lies and right and wrong. She didn't mind Hilda's cross-examination because of her closeness to her new friend, but she would not have taken it kindly if anyone else had asked her questions about herself.

'What's your partner's name?' asked Hilda.

Sarah took out a cigarette and lit it.

'Tony.'

'Where is he from?'

'Oh, he's a Londoner like me. A Londoner born and bred.'

'How often does he service you?'

'You speak as if I were a car. Once a night, actually. And yours?' she added hastily.

'Night and morning.'

'Oh, you're up on me there.'

This was the only occasion during the conversation when Sarah had not lied.

'What do you think of old Blenkinsop?' Hilda asked suddenly.

'I think he's rather sweet but I hate looking him in the face because he's so proverbially ugly.'

Hilda looked suspiciously at Sarah from the corner of her eye. 'You want to watch that man, Blenkinsop. Dr Mackay, on whom everyone in the department dotes, says he's got a schizoid personality disorder. He's an absolute bastard to nurses and cleaners. He sucks up to you because of your educated voice. Do you know what he did the other day?'

Sarah leant over the table, intrigued.

'What did he do?'

'He dropped his doctor's bag on the floor. It was open, and out of it spilled a whole lot of women's lingerie which he'd stolen from clothes-lines.'

Sarah was getting progressively drunk and had hysterical giggles.

'That sounds like the sort of thing Blenkinsop might do. He's such a namby-pamby, old woman. What does he do with these things?'

'Since his wife kicked him out last year, he's been living alone in North London. His Harley Street secretary, Jane Ellis, says he confessed to her that he liked wearing stolen lingerie close to his skin.'

'I must say I find that quite amusing,' said Sarah, 'Do you think he touches himself when he wears these garments?'

'Good God, yes!'

The two women laughed like maniacs.

'It's obvious he fancies you,' said Hilda. 'I bet he has fantasies about you walking over his naked body in stiletto heels.'

'I wouldn't walk over that quivering blubber even if I were paid.'

When Sarah came to work the following morning, she heard a man's and woman's voices raised in anger. The woman's was that of Ingrid, the West Indian cleaner who suffered from high blood pressure. Hilda and Sarah were fond of Ingrid. They liked her loud, coarse laugh and were amused by her hypochondria.

The argument was between her and Blenkinsop.

'I don't care who you is, whether you're an important doctor or a flippin' gravedigger, innit?' shouted Ingrid at the top of her voice. 'Why you have to leave the toilet full of shit all the time? Why you never use the brush to wipe away what you done, innit? It's putting my blood pressure up and when you wipes yourself, you always leaves the paper all over the floor, innit?'

'Your behaviour is unacceptable,' replied Blenkinsop, his voice loud and trembling. 'Your supervisor will be informed about your extreme discourtesy and insolence.'

Ingrid did not return to work the following day. Neither Sarah nor Hilda saw her again.

Blenkinsop's constant absenteeism from the hospital increased dramatically. During the cricket season, he was hardly seen at all. Mackay had to work late into the evening, seeing Blenkinsop's patients.

'Where the hell's Blenkinsop, Hilda?' asked Mackay.

'He phoned in yesterday to say that he was ill.'

'He's always ill!' rasped Mackay. 'Do you know where you'd be most likely to find him?'

'I've no idea. Where?'

'Either at Lord's cricket ground, or in the mortuary, or hanging about in women's back gardens, trying to steal their bloody washing!'

Hilda miraculously managed to keep a straight face.

'Oh, has he got to identify a patient in the mortuary?' she asked, her face awash with mock innocence.

'No!' shouted Mackay. 'He goes in there for his filthy little kicks. It turns him on to fondle dead bodies.'

Hilda mimicked a genteel, Croydon accent. 'We don't do things like that where I come from,' she said. 'We think it's ever so rude.'

* * *

Joan, over whom Sarah had been promoted, was herself promoted without warning, over the heads of Sarah and Hilda, who remained higher clerical officers.

Joan had always disliked Sarah whom she knew was cleverer than she. Joan confided in Hilda her hatred for Sarah and Hilda repeated Joan's words to Sarah in the pub every day at lunch. This resulted in Sarah being cold and cutting towards Joan. Hilda, too, humiliated Joan every time an opportunity arose.

Blenkinsop had fallen hopelessly in love with Sarah but Sarah continued to find him repulsive but amusing on

173

account of his perverse habits. Every evening, she would have her uncle rolling all over the room with laughter, evoked by her anecdotes about Blenkinsop.

It was at that time that Sarah suffered a psychological blow. Joan had wrongfully accused Hilda of stealing condoms from her desk drawer, in front of three giggling, junior doctors. Sarah suggested discussing the matter in a calm and restrained manner. Hilda was so incensed, however, that she gathered all her personal belongings together and dramatically handed in her notice, announcing to everyone she saw, for some reason, that she was a Capricorn and unaccustomed to being publicly slighted. Now, Sarah was without her mate and her job without its charm.

She was relieved that O'Rafferty's six months' assignment in England was coming to a close. He had been posted to Dublin and she would have to find a medical, secretarial job there.

'Dr Blenkinsop, I'm afraid I have some sad news for you.' It was nine-fifteen on a Monday morning.

'Yes?'

'I'm going to live in Dublin. My partner's found a job there.'

Blenkinsop said nothing and sank into a mood of intolerable gloom.

'I see, Sarah,' he muttered after a few moments.

Unbeknown to Sarah, Blenkinsop had developed a morbid and unwholesome obsession about her and had consulted numerous psychiatrists. Because he was aware of her unobtainability, he thought about her throughout his waking hours and her white, ivory skin fuelled his necrophile fantasies.

A group photograph had been taken of the departmental workforce. Sarah was shown smiling, wearing a bright red sweater and a leopard-skin scarf. Blenkinsop had circled

174

her picture and had had it blown up to a size that covered an entire wall in his flat.

In addition to this relatively harmless action, Blenkinsop had purchased a number of black rubber mackintoshes. He would stand in front of Sarah's blown up picture, wearing one of these and would rub himself against it, not daring to sully his feelings for her by actually touching himself.

*   *   *

Once Sarah and O'Rafferty had left for Dublin, Blenkinsop applied for a senior consultancy post in respiratory medicine in the Hospital of Our Holy Redeemer there. Sarah had registered with the only medical, secretarial agency in Dublin, and had given the agency the number of the telephone in the flat which O'Rafferty had bought her. The agency refused to give Blenkinsop her number, until he pleaded with them that he was Sarah's father who had to break the news to her that her mother had died.

'Hullo,' said Sarah.

'Hullo, love,' came a hollow, bleating voice on the line.

'Dr Blenkinsop, how did you find me?'

'I have my ways. Are you looking for work?'

'Yes. I've been sitting by a silent phone for two weeks.'

'Hasn't your agency been in touch with you?'

'No.'

'I'm working in the Hospital of Our Holy Redeemer. We're in urgent need of someone with your skills. When can you start?'

'Well, I can start on Monday.'

'Good,' said Blenkinsop, trying to control the heaviness of his breathing and the shakiness of his voice. He wiped his forehead with his handkerchief and nervously tweaked the knot in his tie.

Marie O'Dwyer had been working in the post to be

allocated to Sarah, for twenty-five years. She was a dedicated worker who stayed overtime to complete the huge workload and even came in at eight o'clock in the morning instead of nine o'clock. Marie was widowed and lonely. Her entire life revolved round the hospital and she went in at weekends as well, to do the only things which made her sad life worth living.

Blenkinsop had taken over as senior consultant from Dr McAdam, a benevolent, white-haired man who had recently retired. Blenkinsop realized that he had to get rid of this dedicated, old lady with the minimum amount of fuss, to make way for Sarah. Because he was a newcomer, he had little influence over the personnel management of the hospital so he took Marie's execution into his own hands.

He waited until ten p.m. on Friday and put a sachet of diamorphine in her bottom drawer. On Monday, he waited for her to take off her coat and put another sachet in her coat pocket. Then he called the head of Personnel into his office and asked Marie to join them. He allowed the head of Personnel to do most of the talking.

'Do you have problems at home, Marie?'

'No. This place has been my home ever since my husband died.'

'This was found in one of your drawers by a cleaner who handed it in to Dr Blenkinsop. Would you explain yourself?' said the personnel manager.

Marie, though dedicated, was not graced with great intelligence.

'I don't even know what it is.'

'It's called heroin,' said Blenkinsop. 'H-E-R-O-I-N. How long have you been on it?'

Marie was in tears.

'I've never taken it in my life. I don't understand.'

'I think you do,' said Blenkinsop. 'Would you go and fetch your overcoat, please.'

Marie had no idea that she was going to be dismissed and it didn't occur to her to check the contents of her coat pockets. She returned to Blenkinsop's office, carrying the coat.

'Turn out your pockets,' he ordered.

She obeyed. She pulled out a gold cross with a broken chain, a string of rosary beads, an unused, lace handkerchief and a sachet of diamorphine. She put all these things on the desk.

'You know what this means, don't you?' said the head of Personnel.

'No.'

'Instant dismissal. Gather your possessions together and do not return to this hospital unless as a patient.'

Marie was so stunned that she obeyed without question. That evening, she went to the banks of the river Liffey, taking a bottle of Paracetamol in one hand and a bottle of milk in the other. She swallowed the contents of the bottle, namely a hundred pills. As she gradually became drowsier and drowsier, she prayed briefly that Blenkinsop's evil soul would find salvation and rolled down the banks of the Liffey into eternal sleep. As yet, Sarah knew nothing about the incident.

* * *

Sarah's aunt, Melissa, had suffered a further deterioration in her health. Word had reached her that her husband was responsible for Sarah's pregnancy. This, combined with worsening disagreements with her children, caused her to drink at least two bottles of gin a day and she had been diagnosed as having terminal cirrhosis of the liver.

Her domestic situation was not helped by the fact that O'Rafferty had allowed her to keep a shotgun by her bed, after receiving threats from Protestant loyalists, who were suspicious of his dubious political connections. After a heavy drinking binge, Melissa had shot the maid bringing her her breakfast, in the chest, just half an inch away from the heart, mistaking her, in her semi-comatose state, for a Protestant loyalist.

O'Rafferty's health, too, had gradually become poor. He had developed a persistent cough over the months.

'I'm worried about that cough of yours,' said Sarah one morning when she was bathing him.

'I've had this cough for a long time now. It must be an allergy.'

O'Rafferty had been smoking over eighty cigarettes a day since hearing about his wife's liver disease. His lingering cough lasted throughout the night, even during sleep and was accompanied by a sensation of pain in the left side of his chest. He was also coughing up blood.

'I'm not going to be at peace until you've consulted a doctor about your cough,' said Sarah.

'I suppose that's because you want me to meet that repulsive man, Blenkinsop, and be treated by him. I can't be doing with a necrophiliac pawing my chest.'

'Never mind about his hobbies,' said Sarah. 'He may be foul and revolting in his activities after work but he is still a brilliant chest specialist.'

'I don't much like the idea of being treated by a Brit either,' said O'Rafferty.

An argument ensued. O'Rafferty eventually agreed to see his family doctor, Dr Ryan, about his complaint which he was convinced was due, either to an allegy, or a form of asthma.

Ryan examined his swarthy but surprisingly pale patient and was dissatisfied with his findings. 'I'm not happy about the sound of your chest and the symptoms you are describing, Mr O'Rafferty,' said Ryan, after putting his examining instruments back into his bag. 'I insist that you see the new English chest specialist at the Hospital of

Our Holy Redeemer. I've sent other patients to him with promising results.'

O'Rafferty was no doctor's ideal patient on account of his murderous temper and irascibility.

'I've heard about that man!' he shouted. 'I'm not going to be shoved on to the hands of a filthy Brit who fucks the bloody dead!'

Dr Ryan laid his hands on O'Rafferty's shoulders and pushed him gently back on to the couch on which he had been examined. 'Come now, Mr O'Rafferty. 'Tis wrong and uncharitable to pass judgement of such an unholy nature on one of God's human beings.'

'He's British,' muttered O'Rafferty.

'And what if he is? He could still save your life.'

'But surely it's only some allergy that I've got, or asthma maybe?'

'I'm not prepared to agree with that. It might easily be something else.'

'What, then?'

'We'll only know the answer to that when you've seen Dr Blenkinsop.'

'Does he see patients privately?'

'Yes, but only in the hospital. He doesn't have rooms off the premises.'

O'Rafferty kept his appointment with Blenkinsop and drove Sarah home in the van which she had left in the hospital car park. Just before they left, Sarah asked: 'How did you get on with old Blenkinsop? What did he say was wrong with you?'

O'Rafferty turned on the ignition. The engine started running. 'Sarah, you've told me an awful lot about this man. You said that he was very repulsive and weird but Jaysus – I always thought that up to now you had to be exaggerating.'

'Why, what happened?'

179

'I thought the man was a bit of an iron.* Do you realize that he tried to put his finger up my hole! I said that's not the sort of thing that one fellow does to another.'

'That shows how little you know about medicine, Uncle Seamus. A doctor is supposed to cover all parts of the body during a medical examination. These people adhere to the saying: "If you don't put your finger in it, you'll put your foot in it." '

O'Rafferty and Sarah laughed and embraced. Sarah clung to her lover with even more abandon than before, because she had a morbid instinct that fate would shortly be taking him from her.

Blenkinsop was looking down at the car park from his consulting room. The sun had gone behind a cloud and he happened to get up to adjust the Venetian blind to get more evening light.

He watched the embrace between the sick man and the pretty, young woman and his cheeks were covered with tears of joy. He knew what he had to do to make Sarah his.

'What did Blenkinsop say?' asked Sarah.

'He made me have a chest X-ray and told me to come back next Wednesday.'

Sarah could not eat or sleep until Wednesday. She dreaded finding out what the X-ray would show, and because of O'Rafferty's worsening cough, she feared that it would be positive for cancer.

It was Tuesday afternoon. Blenkinsop slapped O'Rafferty's chest X-ray into a slot on an illuminated wall in a windowless room. The doctor's hideous face broke into a broad, semi-toothless smile. He made a note of his diagnosis, 'Primary carcinoma of the left lung. Treatment: immediate lobectomy within about two weeks followed by radiotherapy.'

*Iron: outmoded Irish slang word for homosexual.

He produced a bottle of Tippex erasing fluid and whited out the name 'Seamus O'Rafferty' and 'DOB 22.06.20'. He included the X-ray with the other X-rays to be shown to his students on the next X-ray round.

His students were a little in awe of him because of his refined, English accent.

'Well, Mr O'Connor,' said Blenkinsop affably, 'can you provide me with a diagnosis on this patient?' He slotted O'Rafferty's film onto the illuminated wall.

'The film would suggest a primary carcinoma of the left lung. Is that not right, sir?'

'Yes, Mr O'Connor, that is absolutely right. Well done. Can you suggest the prognosis?'

'I think the prognosis is quite reasonable, sir. The carcinoma is only in its primary stage but secondaries could develop without immediate surgery and radio-therapy.'

'That is correct, Mr O'Connell.'

'O'Connor.'

'Oh, I'm so sorry, Mr O'Connor.'

The older man patted the student on the back.

'I can see that you are going to go far in your chosen field.'

'That's generous of you to say so, sir.'

*　*　*

O'Rafferty kept his appointment with Blenkinsop the following day.

'Sit down, would you please, Mr O'Rafferty,' said the doctor.

O'Rafferty sat down and Blenkinsop immediately recognized the fear in his face.

'Don't dawdle on this one, doc. How long have I got?'

Blenkinsop pushed his chair away from his desk and stretched out his arms. 'How long have you got? But, my dear fellow, your X-ray is perfectly normal. In fact, I can show it to you, together with the radiographer's typed report. Look – it says: "Heart size normal. Lungs clear." There at the bottom, are the radiographer's initials followed by the typist's initials in small letters.'

'I still don't see why my cough's getting worse, doc.'

'Well, it must be something you're allergic to. Maybe it's horses. Maybe it's something as simple as house dust mite. I'm writing a letter to our ear, nose and throat surgeons suggesting an allergy test. Your lungs are perfectly all right.'

'Why am I coughing up blood?' asked O'Rafferty aggressively.

'It is quite common to cough up blood if someone's allergic to something,' replied Blenkinsop.

O'Rafferty's ignorance of the fact that Blenkinsop had shown him a bogus X-ray, combined with his enormous relief, caused him to get irritable.

'Now, look here, doc, I don't want any goddamn allergy tests. I've other things to be doing. Sorry to have taken up your time.'

Blenkinsop got up and opened the door for his patient, smiling slyly.

'Not at all. That is what I am here for – to allow you to take up my time. Kindly pick up your bill from my nurse as you go out.'

O'Rafferty did so. The cost of the two consultations plus the X-ray, so called, was five hundred pounds.

'Oh, do call again,' Blenkinsop said as O'Rafferty was walking downstairs. 'That is if you think I can be of any further help.'

Sarah was waiting for him in the van. He was convulsed with tears of relief.

'I'm clear, my little lassie, I'm clear!' he shouted.

Blenkinsop watched them from his consulting room

182

through the slits of the Venetian blind, and basked in his power to ruin and manipulate the lives of others.

He snapped the proper X-ray back on to the wall and turned off the light. Then he began to touch himself.

* * *

Within the next ten days, Melissa took her life, partly because she knew that she was terminally ill, and partly because of the rumours which she had heard about her husband and her niece. Sarah did everything in her power to comfort her uncle during the ensuing weeks and succeeded, if only to some extent, in cheering him up. His cigarette consumption rose from eighty to a hundred a day, his cough worsened and he had to strain himself to suck air into his lungs.

One morning, he stormed into Blenkinsop's office while he was dictating to Sarah. O'Rafferty was initially struck by how prim and proper his mistress looked as she was taking dictation, with her legs crossed and her skirt pulled demurely over her knees. It was a pose he had never seen her in before and he was immediately touched by her purity and fidelity.

'Come on, doc. I want a word with you,' he said, kicking the door wide open and allowing it to bang against an occasional table, on which stood a photograph of Blenkinsop's debauched mother.

Sarah sprang to her feet.

'Would you mind waiting outside, sir. Perhaps you could leave your name and telephone number and Dr Blenkinsop will ring you when he is free.'

Her attempted concealment of their relationship touched O'Rafferty and her brisk, crisp efficiency endeared Blenkinsop to her even more.

O'Rafferty wrote his name and telephone number down on the back of an envelope. Blenkinsop rang him at home later that day, and suggested that he come in for a repeat chest X-ray.

Again the same procedure was repeated. The next X-ray still showed that O'Rafferty had primary cancer of the left lung. Once more, Blenkinsop exchanged the X-ray with a perfectly normal one, abusing the computer to log O'Rafferty's name and date of birth at the bottom of the X-ray.

'Mr O'Rafferty, you can see for yourself and you can read the X-ray report yet again. As yet, your lungs are entirely normal, but you risk getting into a lot of trouble later on if you don't cut down on your tobacco intake. You told me that you were up to a hundred cigarettes a day. Surely, you must realize that this is quite disgraceful, as well as being downright dangerous. No wonder you have a bad cough and cough all through the night as well. If you don't give up smoking now, you do run the risk of getting lung cancer. Do you think that it would give me pleasure to show you an X-ray that was abnormal due to lung cancer?'

'No, doc,' O'Rafferty muttered.

'You do see sense, then? You do see how distressing it would be for me, as well as for you, were your X-ray to be abnormal?'

'Yes, doc.'

'So, will you agree to give up smoking today?'

'Yes, I will, doc.'

O'Rafferty chewed nicotine-containing chewing gum from that day onwards. Still, he was coughing and choking all day and all night. He became depressed because of Melissa's suicide and because the pleasure of lighting a cigarette was being denied him. Further, his moody temperament was upsetting Sarah who was heavily pregnant.

'I've got an idea, Uncle Seamus.' They were sitting by the imitation, log fire in Sarah's flat.

184

'What have you in mind?' asked O'Rafferty. His tone was flat and disinterested.

'I'm told the IRA has organized a rally next Saturday. Apparently, they want a female singer to sing, "A Rebel Hand Set the Heather Blazing".'

'How did you find this out?'

'From Flossie who cleans the lavatories in our department. She's a republican.'

'So, where is this going to be?'

'She said it would be in the Wolfe Tone Hotel. There's a big ballroom there. That's where the rally will be. They'll be collecting money for the Catholics in the north.'

O'Rafferty was mildly drunk and felt better.

'That's not a bad idea, is it lassie? Can you still sing, "A Rebel Hand Set the Heather Blazing"?'

'Yes.'

'All right. Sing it, then.'

When sober, Sarah had a singing voice which she boasted reminded listeners of silvery wine flowing through a spaceship. However, when drunk, the less charitable among them occasionally commented that she sounded like a combination of a banshee being buried alive and a bus changing gear. The main feature of her singing voice was that it was head-splittingly loud, so much so, that not just rooms, but buildings would be emptied, once she started singing. A dying patient at Battersea General, whom Sarah had gone to comfort to create a favourable impression when she was drunk, unwisely asked her to sing. She decided to sing, *There's Hole in my Bucket*. The patient died almost as soon as Sarah opened her mouth.

When Sarah sang the rebel song to O'Rafferty, a tide of nostalgia and memories of her as a little girl swept through him. He wept. Sarah had never seen a man cry before. The sight of her uncle in tears alarmed her.

'What's the matter, Uncle Seamus?'

'All I want out of life is to be able to live to see our child and I hope it's going to be a girl.'

'What are you talking about? Both your X-rays are OK. You've stopped smoking. You'll live to see our great grandchildren.'

'I'm not so sure. There's something sinister and slippery about that fellow, Blenkinsop. He always talks as if he's trying to hide something.'

'I think you've misjudged him,' said Sarah, whose fatal weakness was to have blind trust in anyone who flattered her. 'He's always been very nice to me but I do see in him a marked lack of confidence and self-esteem.'

'You're not as streetwise as I am, lassie. I know a manipulating liar when I see one.'

'Your judgement is all wrong. I'm sure Dr Blenkinsop's not a liar or a manipulator. If he were, he wouldn't be allowed to practise. He may be a fussy, little, old woman in his ways but I'm sure he wouldn't hurt a fly.'

'It almost sounds as if you fancied the bastard,' said O'Rafferty.

'Did the actress, Madge Kendal, fancy the Elephant Man?' asked Sarah.

'No, I should think she didn't but that fellow, Blenkinsop is so hideous that he'd make the Elephant Man look like Rudolph Valentino.'

'We do have one thing in common, though,' said Sarah.

'Oh, Jaysus, what?'

'We are both fascinated by medicine and death.'

'Well, when I croak, I'm sure you'll both have a field day. Does he go in for male stiffs as well as females?'

Sarah gave her uncle a smack on the back of his hand in mock anger. 'Don't be so disgusting, Seamus O'Rafferty!'

* * *

The turnout at the IRA rally was enormous. The republican flag was placed in the centre of the platform next to a microphone. There were two hundred hardened supporters of the IRA there, a few of whom made stirring, but rasping speeches with harsh, Dublin accents.

The people in the audience were dressed in paramilitary clothing with their faces obscured by balaclavas. The male members of the audience had had quite a lot to drink before the rally and were high-spirited and frisky.

O'Rafferty and Sarah mounted the platform. O'Rafferty seized the microphone and spoke uninhibitedly with his hand on Sarah's shoulder.

'*Erin go bragh!*' he shouted.

'*Erin go bragh!*' the audience bellowed unanimously.

'I would like to introduce my daughter, Sarah who is with child, God bless her! She has come here tonight to sing, *A Rebel Hand Set the Heather Blazing.*'

The audience applauded which gave Sarah extreme self-confidence, bringing out her pronounced exhibitionist streak. She was stone cold sober. She had on an emerald green vest which clung tightly to her body, accentuating her swollen stomach, a pair of matching, green shorts with white, fishnet tights and green, patent, high-heeled sandals. Her long, blonde hair, coiffed in ringlets, spread over her shoulders and covered most of her back. On her left wrist was a gold watch which O'Rafferty had given her, and three bangles, coloured green, white and orange, adorned her right wrist.

She took hold of the microphone. The fiddlers and drummers started to play the introduction to the song and the drummers struck up a thundering climax just before the last verse.

Sarah sang the rousing, if dirge-like song, moving sensually, almost making her performance seem like an act of fornication.

187

By the oak as the sun was setting
On the bright May meadows of Shelmaliere,
A rebel hand set the heather blazing
And brought the neighbours from far and near.

Then Father Murphy from County Wexford
Shinned up the rocks with a warring cry.
'Arm, arm' he shouted 'for I've come to lead you,
For Ireland's freedom to fight and die.'

We lost out 'gainst the coming slaying.
Our heroes floundering stood back to back.
Then British tyrants seized Father Murphy
And burned his body upon the rack.

God grant you glory, brave Father Murphy,
And hope in Heaven for all your men,
For the cause which called you may come tomorrow,
In another fight for the Green again.

O'Rafferty was the only person in the ballroom not wearing a balaclava. As he listened to Sarah, looking proudly and lovingly at her swollen stomach, tears of adoration flowed down his cheeks, partly because he knew instinctively that he would not live to see his child.

The room was in uproar. The audience had been swaying from right to left and from left to right again, in rhythm to the classic republican song. Sarah was riding on the crest of a wave of almost clinical megalomania. As the people in the audience chanted her name, she flounced, not without grace, backwards and forwards on the platform, shaking her head in rhythm with her movements, allowing her mane of golden hair to whip each side of her face.

O'Rafferty was seized by an attack of coughing. He

leant forward and clutched his chest in an attempt to assuage the pain. A man in a balaclava came forward and slapped him on the back but his coughing only grew worse.

'I'll drive you home, Uncle Seamus,' said Sarah.

'I'll be all right. Your singing was hypnotic. You were wonderful.'

'Aren't I always wonderful? Come on, it's time I took you home.'

On the way home, O'Rafferty could hardly suck air into his lungs but he was able to speak.

'Sarah?'

'Speaking, dear.'

O'Rafferty laughed which brought on another coughing attack.

'Seriously, Sarah, I'm not happy with Blenkinsop. He gives me the creeps. I must have a second opinion.'

Sarah had been worried all along but she wasn't able to tell herself that she was worried. She had forced herself to believe Blenkinsop's words that there was nothing wrong with her uncle.

'Tomorrow, I'll ring Dr Ryan,' she said. 'He'll find another chest specialist for you. If you want my opinion, I think you're suffering from morbid hypochondria.'

O'Rafferty felt too ill to get angry.

'I'm going to another specialist, whether you like it, or not,' he stated.

Dr Ryan, briefly examined his patient and was adamant that his condition had deteriorated since they had last met.

'I regret having sent you to Dr Blenkinsop in the first place. Do you know what I heard the other day?' said Dr Ryan.

'I'm not interested in what you heard the other fockin' day! All I want is for my chest to stop feeling like raw meat and my coughing to stop!' gasped O'Rafferty.

189

'It's all right. I've already rung Dr O'Shaughnessy, another chest specialist. He said he'll be able to fit you in at six o'clock this evening.'

O'Rafferty calmed down a little. 'Thanks, doc. Just out of interest, what did you hear the other day about Blenkinsop?'

'I heard that he desperately wanted to get rid of his secretary before his new secretary came, so he left a sachet of heroin in her drawer and another in the pocket of her coat. Then he sent for the head of Personnel and dismissed her. The worst of it's to come. She killed herself. She was an old lady coming up for retirement. Can you imagine?'

O'Rafferty knew exactly who Blenkinsop was and what he wanted. Although countless numbers of innocent people had been maimed and murdered under his command in what he considered to be a war, he seethed with anger because an elderly, Irish lady had been cruelly manipulated by an Englishman and driven to suicide. He also bitterly resented Blenkinsop's twisted idolatry of Sarah.

* * *

Dr O'Shaughnessy's consulting room was bleak. It had dark brown, oak-panelled walls and a window set high up on the wall, making it look like a prison cell. Apart from a solitary painting of Patrick Pearse,* the dark walls were bare.

The consultant himself looked pasty, tired and humourless and even his voice sounded like that of someone announcing a bereavement. O'Rafferty and Sarah sat before him. Sarah was holding her uncle's hand and stroking it.

'Sure, I'm not one to beat about the bush, Mr O'Rafferty,' said O'Shaughnessy, 'so you might as well hear it straight away.'

---

*Patrick Pearse: a Gaelic scholar and Irish rebel, who played a significant part in the 1916 uprising. He was eventually shot.

190

'Well, get on with it. What is it?' said O'Rafferty impatiently.

'Mr O'Rafferty, the film brought to me this afternoon shows that you are terminally ill.'

'Terminally ill? Terminally bloody ill?'

'I fear so, sir. If you would like to come into the other room, I'll show you your X-ray.'

Sarah was in too great a state of shock to show any emotion. She took hold of O'Rafferty's arm and guided him through into the other room, following O'Shaughnessy.

O'Rafferty was almost too weak to stand. He sat in a leather-studded chair and gaped at the X-ray which, without medical knowledge, was incomprehensible.

'OK, doc. How long have I got?'

'Only a few weeks, I'm afraid, sir. Your left lung is riddled with cancer, as well as about a quarter of your right lung. This is a fairly unusual phenomenon.'

'But Dr Blenkinsop, whom I saw fairly recently, said my last two X-rays were completely normal. He said that I was coughing because of an allergy,' gasped O'Rafferty.

O'Shaughnessy shuffled from one foot to another. 'I fear that Dr Blenkinsop is neither an honest man, nor a man worthy of practising medicine. This, of course, must not go beyond this room. Sometimes, British consultants working over here are excellent diagnosticians. Blenkinsop's been in trouble with the Garda recently for pedalling recreational medication.'

'I'm not interested in whether or not he's been pedalling recreational medication!' rasped O'Rafferty. 'I'm not ready to die and I demand to have a lung transplant.'

'Lungs do not come easily, sir,' answered O'Shaughnessy, as he wiped the sweat from his forehead. 'They're not like vegetables.'

O'Rafferty was almost in tears and Sarah had started to sob hysterically.

'Isn't there anything you can do to prolong my life?'

'No, sir. I'm afraid not. Had you come earlier, there would have been quite some hope, but now it's only a matter of weeks before you are started on morphine. Are you covered by private insurance?'

'Yes, but only for outpatient consultations. I haven't got private hospital clearance.'

'Then I very much fear that when the time comes, you will have to be admitted to the Hospital of Our Holy Redeemer.'

'All right. I suppose I'll be far too ill to kick Blenkinsop in the balls, let alone recognize him,' muttered O'Rafferty.

* * *

For the next few days, Sarah was racked by an unbreakable cloud of despair. She hired a live-in nurse to look after O'Rafferty and, like Melissa, she drank herself into oblivion, using vodka which did not smell on her breath.

Every weekday she went to her office, pretending that she knew nothing of Blenkinsop's cold, calculating evil, and got on with her work. This took her mind off O'Rafferty's illness and as she had been indoctrinated by the Protestant work ethic, she carried out Blenkinsop's orders and worked as hard and as fast as she could to earn her salary.

The alternative of getting a job in another hospital was daunting. Medical, secretarial work was hard to get, particularly in Dublin, so she remained quiet and attended to her duties with clinical efficiency.

Blenkinsop walked into her office one day, believing that she would be his to have. He approached her as she was typing, giving her a mirthless, semi-toothless grin.

'Hullo, love. What are you hoping for – a little boy or a little girl?'

Sarah kept her eyes on her keys and continued typing without looking up.

'A girl,' she muttered curtly.

Blenkinsop breathed his halitosis into her face, making her shudder.

'I've always preferred little boys to little girls. Have you chosen your godparents yet?'

'Nope!'

'Oh, Sarah, I know that you are glued conscientiously to your work and that you are unusually industrious, but you could still try to be a bit more friendly. I do have very strong feelings about you – so much so that I would like to volunteer to be a godfather to your child.'

Sarah knew that if she were thrown out of her current post, she would have no one to support her financially. Her parents had disowned her when they heard that she had been working for the IRA and she was too proud to suggest herself for weeks on end at Mulligan Manor.

One evening after five o'clock, she was so miserable that she decided to ring her cousin, Varinia, who lived in Oxfordshire with her husband and three daughters. Even in her childhood, Sarah had worshipped Varinia, who was invaluable towards people in distress. Varinia could defuse even the most dastardly atmospheres or situations by cracking brilliantly witty jokes which broke them up instantly, thereby converting her approachers, from a spirit of despair and rage, to calm. Varinia had an attractive face. She had shoulder-length brown hair and a widow's peak. Sarah had always been dependent on her during crises and referred to her as 'the goddess of wit'.

After Blenkinsop had gone home, she reached for the office telephone and dialled Varinia's number.

'Varinia?'

'No, sorry, it's Judith.'

'I need to speak to Varinia,' shouted Sarah, now in tears.

Sarah thought for a moment that Varinia was out and

her suppressed rage, grief and fear caused her to let out an agonizing, wailing scream.

'Varinia! Varinia! Varinia! – Get her for Christ's sake!'

'Cool it, caller,' said Judith, a ten-year-old child who had inherited her mother's precocity. 'Mummy! There's a call for you. I don't know but I suspect it's that mad Sarah. It couldn't be anyone else.'

Sarah relaxed as soon as she heard Varinia speaking to her daughter.

'You said all those things with the mouthpiece uncovered. Have you no manners?'

'Varinia! Varinia! Varinia! Help me!'

Varinia's comforting voice came on to the line.

'Hullo, Sarah! What's the matter, old girl? And what's all this extraordinary business about you working for the IRA?'

'It's not true. I've got nothing to do with it. I've got terrible, ghastly news.'

'What news, old girl?'

'Uncle Seamus is terminally ill with cancer of the lungs.'

There was a slight pause. 'Oh, God, when did you find this out?' asked Varinia, who was fond of O'Rafferty and amused by his domestic tantrums, but ignorant of his connection with the IRA.

'A chest specialist called O'Shaughnessy, diagnosed the illness. And there's this evil man, Blenkinsop.'

'Blenkinsop? Who's he? I've never heard of him.'

'It's too complicated to explain the situation over the telephone. I need to see you.'

'You really are extraordinary, old girl. Why won't you talk to me about this man, Blenkinsop?'

'I can't. I just can't. Oh, Varinia, I don't know what's to become of me.'

'Come on, Sarah. I know you're hiding something. You can tell Varinia. She won't tell anyone.'

194

Varinia's kind words caused Sarah to cry even more.

'It's all right, old girl. Never fear; Varinia's here.'

'I don't even know how to tell the children. Uncle Seamus is a bit like King Lear.'

'I beg your pardon. You're not drunk, are you?'

'No. The question is – which of his three daughters most resembles Cordelia?'

'I think you'll find that that family's somewhat short of Cordelias,' replied Varinia stridently.

Sarah had an attack of mirthless, hysterical laughter. 'Oh, Varinia, you don't know how much good you've done me during this short conversation. You've made me laugh and the gift of laughter is worth all the alcohol in the world.'

'Well, don't have too much of that, whatever you do.'

'Varinia, you may not realize this but you've given me courage.'

'Anything to oblige, old girl. Give me a ring again next time you're feeling gloomy.'

That evening, Sarah approached her uncle's bedside with an unforced smile. 'You're going to survive, Seamus,' she said.

'You sound convinced. Come on. Get into bed with me.'

* * *

O'Rafferty was becoming weaker and weaker. His former handsomeness had been annihilated by his disease. There came a time when it was necessary for Sarah and him to sleep in separate rooms. He was already being injected with ten milligrams of morphine at regular intervals, and the nurse sitting in his room had to turn him over several times a night.

O'Rafferty realized that he was not covered for residential nursing treatment and was terrified that the bill would be sent to Sarah after his death. He called her to his bedside, his once raucous voice now a pathetic, little bleat.

'I think I'm ready for it, now.'

'Ready for what?'

'To be moved to the Hospital of Our Holy Redeemer. I don't care whether Blenkinsop's there or not, as long as I get my morphine, and as long as I can be looked after.'

Sarah rushed out of the room in tears. She composed herself and came back.

'Your illness is just a passing thing. You're going to live,' she said, not very convincingly.

* * *

An ambulance arrived outside Sarah's home one Monday morning. O'Rafferty, who had become skeletal, was carried into it on a stretcher. Sarah got into the ambulance and sat near him, holding his hand throughout the journey.

Once at the Hospital of Our Holy Redeemer, O'Rafferty was lifted on to a wheelchair and carried in the lift to the fifth floor, where there were two wards for the terminally ill, segregated by sex.

Sarah waited for the nurses to settle him in, and went out to buy grapes for him, they being the only things he enjoyed eating.

The nurses pulled the curtains round the bed in which O'Rafferty lay, to give him a blanket bath. Sarah decided to talk to another patient on the ward who was staring melancholically into space. For some reason, perhaps morbid curiosity, Sarah sat by the man's bedside. A drip was being fed into him intravenously, and two other cellophane bags were being used to collect urine and solid waste from his body.

'So how are you doing, sir?' asked Sarah inanely, and immediately regretted her question, when the patient explained to her at length precisely how he thought he was doing.

'When I get taken, I shall be put in a box. A deep grave will be dug for me. My body will rot in the earth and as it decomposes, the worms and maggots will eat what is left of my flesh and pick my bones clean. My soul will not go to Heaven. It will stay with my body while it is being consumed by the maggots and it will remain with my body until the crack of doom.'

Sarah was struck by a vicious attack of melancholia. She felt suicidal, as she tried in vain to search for appropriate words.

'Will it, now?' she eventually managed to mutter.

Sarah was at an advantage, in that she was working in an office close to O'Rafferty's ward. She spent her tea, coffee and lunch breaks in his company, holding and stroking his hand.

Every Thursday morning, Blenkinsop, accompanied by his senior registrar and senior house officers, would go on his ward round. He greeted each patient with a pseudo-enthusiastic, breathless 'Hi!' and moved on to the next patient, without bothering to listen to the previous patient's reply.

Blenkinsop eventually came to O'Rafferty and saw Sarah, half sitting and half lying on top of his bed, weeping.

'How are you feeling, Mr O'Rafferty?' Blenkinsop took phenomenal pleasure in offering patients the putter when their golf balls were in a bunker.

O'Rafferty tried to raise his head and shoulders but even this mild exertion exhausted him. He tried to open his mouth and struggled to find his words. Eventually, he spoke.

'The IRA is going to get you, you filthy, stinking bastard!'

Then he lay down and held Sarah to his chest.

Blenkinsop managed to catch up with the charge nurse, Bridget McDermitt.

'Was there something you wanted, Dr Blenkinsop?'

'If there wasn't, I'd hardly be walking towards you, would I?'

'There's no need to be sarcastic. What do you want?'

Blenkinsop ran his hand through his ridiculous-looking wig. 'I want to discuss the patient in Bed 5, Mr O'Rafferty. He has just informed me that he wishes to die as soon as possible, rather than wait in pain until the end. Euthanasia is legal, provided that a consent form is signed by the patient, the next of kin and the other necessary authorities. This has all been taken in hand.'

'Can you show me the filled-in forms?'

'Doubting my word, are you? I have the power to throw you out of here. That will teach you to question my judgement.'

Bridget hated this man with a homicidal ferocity and struggled to keep her temper, which was harder for her than to hold four Rottweilers on paper leads.

'All right. What are my orders?'

'When you give Mr O'Rafferty his midday injection, you will increase his morphine level to 200 milligrams. If you fail, I can get rid of you on a possession of illegal drugs rap. I've been through the drawers in your office and I've found diamorphine in there.'

'In other words, you've set me up?'

'No, no, love. Not in other words; these are the perfect ones.'

Bridget made a decision to ignore his order. Blenkinsop walked off the ward and broke wind as he did so, causing the place to stink of school kitchens.

'Sarah, my little girl.'

'Yes, Uncle Seamus.'

'I've got a feeling I won't make it through the night. Will you do something for me?'

'Of course I will. What do you want me to do?'

'Just drive over to the house and fetch the republican flag which you'll find in the top drawer in my study,'

'I'll do that for you. I'll bring it to you during my break at eleven. And just remember another thing – you're not going to die in the night. You'll die when I tell you to. No earlier, no later.'

Sarah appeared the following morning, carrying the republican flag. She could see that O'Rafferty was awake and was goaded on by the faint, muffled cheers of other patients, many of them staunch nationalists who saw the flag.

A wave of manic exhibitionism, temporarily drowning her gloom, surged through Sarah. She twirled the flag around her and waved it from left to right with the agility of a matador. Then she began to sing, inviting everyone on the ward to join her.

Take it down from the mast, o ye traitors.
It's the flag we republicans claim.
It can never belong to Free-Staters,
Who have wrought on it nothing but shame.

So then leave it to those who are willing,
To uphold it in war as in peace.
It is they who intend to do killing,
Until England's tyrannies cease.

It was at this point that O'Rafferty feebly joined in the singing. Sarah went to his bedside and draped the flag over his bed. O'Rafferty sang the first verse of the song which comprised the chorus.

Suddenly, he stopped singing and gasped desperately for breath. He reached out for assistance.

'Sarah, help me!'

Sarah held both his hands together and rubbed them

as they felt like blocks of ice. She bent over and kissed him on the mouth.

Suddenly, O'Rafferty let out a horrendous death rattle. Blood spurted on to Sarah's dress and on to the flag. Sarah pulled the flag over his face and wept.

She knew that the only way to keep her sanity would be to immerse herself in her work. She walked down the corridor, her senses numb and entered her office. She found Blenkinsop sitting at her desk. She decided, in the interests of her being solvent, to be civil to him.

'The phone's been ringing non-stop,' said Blenkinsop. 'Where have you been?'

'To the offices of Personnel. They asked me to give them my income tax form.'

'All right, all right. Please see that it doesn't happen again.'

'Yes, Dr Blenkinsop.'

Throughout the following weeks, Blenkinsop's adoration of Sarah became more complicated. He could tell by the aura about her that his adulation was not requited. He had hoped to be able to comfort her and cause her to get round to loving him, but she was too abrupt to give him the courage to say that he wished to embark on an affair with her.

He felt particularly close to her as her pregnancy progressed and because he was mad, he pretended that he was the father of her unborn child. Sometimes, he would look through the keyhole on her office door where she wept silently. In time, his adulation gradually turned to malicious, destructive jealousy and he made up his mind to get rid of Sarah.

He was haunted by her very presence and the factor haunting him most was his inability to determine whether he adored her or despised her. He decided, purely in his own interests, that Sarah should be removed as quickly as possible. The facts that her full income came from the hospital alone, and that medical, secretarial work was particularly hard to come by, were of no interest to him.

At first, Sarah had no idea of the thoughts invading Blenkinsop's mind. Gradually, she began to notice that he wasn't being as friendly as he had been before her bereavement. Sometimes, he would come into her office without greeting her, and would only speak to her to give her curt orders. Now that even he was obviously turning against her, her entire mental strength began to break down. Had she not been pregnant, she would have taken her life.

Blenkinsop did what he always did when wishing to have an employee removed. He sent for the overworked head of Personnel. Then he called Sarah into his office. The same terror-inspiring tactic was used as in the case of Marie O'Dwyer. Blenkinsop and the head of Personnel sat on one side of a shiny, oak desk and Sarah was asked to sit opposite them.

'Do you know why we've called you here?' asked Blenkinsop, running his hands through his wig which had inadvertently become dislodged.

'No.'

'We neither of us feel it appropriate that you work in this hospital.'

'What the hell do you mean? You have always said yourself that my work was excellent.'

The head of Personnel entered the conversation. 'You are heavily pregnant but you are not married to the father of your baby.'

Sarah stood up and banged her fist on the edge of the oak desk. 'So you think that's your bloody business, do you?'

'I've got a suggestion to make, Sarah,' said Blenkinsop. 'This hospital does not cover for unmarried employees taking maternity leave. We will keep you, only provided that you are prepared to have a termination of pregnancy by caesarean section.'

Sarah hated this man so much that she would have killed him outright had she been armed.

'I'll play your filthy little game, which like all games has to be played according to the rules. What's behind your rubbishy, blackmailing tactics?'

'Please understand, Dr Blenkinsop likes you,' said the head of Personnel feebly.

'Likes? Likes? Don't give me that! He wanted to be the father of my unborn child and he's seething with jealousy.'

'Now, you know that's not true, Sarah,' muttered Blenkinsop.

'You've no business to be psychologically beating up a pregnant woman, recently bereaved. What's all this in aid of?'

Blenkinsop moved his chair forward to enable him to rest his elbows on his desk. 'We are both worried about you, Sarah.'

'If it's only me you're worried about, might I suggest that your other problems and worries must be somewhat remote? Why are you worried?'

'Is it true that you are a member of the IRA?'

'No, it certainly isn't. Where did you get that fatuous information from?'

Blenkinsop leaned forward and gave Sarah a sly, conspirational smile. 'Word gets round, doesn't it, love?'

'Kindly don't call me "love". It's proverbially common.'

Blenkinsop ignored her barbed tongue.

'After your uncle's body was collected by the beagle and his team...'

'Don't you mean the beadle? A beagle's a dog.'

'What I am trying to get at is that you were seen in the mortuary.'

202

'It's not a question of my having been seen. I saw you. You had pulled my uncle's body out of a drawer and I saw you lying on top of it, wearing a revolting, black rubber mackintosh, saying, "What's close to Sarah, is attractive to me".'

The head of Personnel cleared her throat and Blenkinsop's face became like an overripe beetroot.

'Oh, no, no! You're fantasizing again, love,' he muttered, adding, 'What we are really trying to tell you is that you are unsound in mind, and it is not hospital policy to give leave to unmarried women who are pregnant. We have arranged for a replacement next Monday, so effectively, this is your last week working here.'

Just then, the head of Personnel glared at Sarah. Sarah glared back at her tormentor's eyes until a few moments had passed. The head of Personnel blushed and looked away.

Sarah rose to her feet, trembling with rage. 'You'll be sorry for your cruelty, Blenkinsop, so sorry you'll wish you'd never been born. And don't think I'm ignorant of the fact that your mother was a whore. The whole hospital knows about that. On top of that, it's your vicious jealousy that I am a victim of. You are nothing in comparison with Seamus O'Rafferty. Take a look at yourself. No woman would wish to screw you, even for a five-figure sum.'

Sarah exited, slamming the door behind her.

She was not entirely desperate. Although O'Rafferty was dead, she was proud to be carrying his seed. She also planned the revenge, which she felt was right, against Blenkinsop.

Before O'Rafferty's admission to hospital, he told Sarah that he wasn't going to live until Christmas, so he said that he would give her her Christmas present prematurely. He had given her a Colt .38 revolver and had an instinct that Blenkinsop would be its target.

Every evening before going to sleep, Sarah would summon the spirit of her hero and idol, Sir Jasper Montrose. 'O, Jas who hailest from the Carpathian Mountains and, who art born half Cossack and half bear, give me the strength to conquer the evil and reprobate Blenkinsop. Help me to do what is best in the interests of thy supreme justice. Help me to find my true honour in observing thy divine will.'

When she had finished, she rose to her feet and a sudden current of comforting warmth surged through her body. She knew that her social prognosis was poor, but she was comforted by the fact that Sir Jasper's spirit was walking by her side, and would see to it that no harm would come to her child.

For the next few weeks, Sarah kept a low profile but because she had no money, she managed to steal tins of food from supermarkets. She kept her loot in stock and estimated that she had stolen enough to feed her baby for at least two months.

She neglected herself. Her shock of tumbling, blonde hair was unwashed and to keep it away from her face, she dragged it on top of her head with a plastic comb. Her tangled hair framed her pale, shrunken face and her flashing blue eyes had lost their allure and had retreated into her skull, like dead fish on a slab.

She wore a black, medieval friar's cloak, its hood covering most of her face, and a heavy, black shawl over her cloak. The shawl had been stolen with Artful Dodger agility from a woman laying down flowers in the graveyard, when she had been paying her daily homage at her uncle's graveside. Even the flowers she brought had been stolen from people's gardens.

Sometimes, she would sit at street corners in affluent parts of Dublin and beg. When well-meaning bystanders gave her coins, she would express thanks in a heavy English accent, which astonished them and caused them to think that they had had a drink too many.

Sarah estimated that she would go into labour some time within the following two weeks, and that Blenkinsop's murder would have to take place as soon as possible.

Very few, if any, knew this strange-looking beggar with the weird English accent. Sarah was alone, unnoticed and had few friends. Nor did she think she needed them, provided she continued to wear the gold locket in which she kept Sir Jasper Montrose's photograph.

*   *   *

On 30 November, coincidentally the birthday of one of Sarah's more incongruous heroes, Sir Winston Churchill, there appeared a bizarre story on the front page of the *Irish Times*.

'Beggar with English accent guns down English doctor in hospital lecture hall', said the headline.

Eileen O'Rafferty, who had been kind and supportive to Sarah at O'Rafferty's republican funeral, was astounded when she picked up the newspaper, laid out with all the other newspapers on the dining room table. She read on.

In a lecture hall at the Hospital of Our Holy Redeemer, an English doctor and specialist in respiratory medicine was shot dead by a pregnant woman with an English accent. The woman advanced uninterrupted towards Dr Peter Blenkinsop, shouting, 'Your time's up, Blenkinsop. You're a vile, vicious, vindictive bastard. You are a murderer, a lecher and an utterly disgusting necrophiliac!'

The woman's weapon, a gold-plated Colt .38 revolver, held six bullets in its chamber and all bullets were pumped into the doctor's body at close range.

'Dr Blenkinsop was disliked,' said a hospital spokesman. 'It is thought that the late Seamus O'Rafferty, who was given a formal IRA funeral, had been one of his patients.'

Dr Blenkinsop's body will be collected by his former wife, Alexandra and his son and daughter, Mark and Isabella, and flown to London later this week, prior to internment on British soil.

Eileen sprang to her feet shouting, 'I've got to find my cousin!' She leapt into her Fiat and drove through the streets of Dublin, heading for the Hospital of Our Holy Redeemer, to find out whether Sarah had escaped or given herself up.

Her journey was abortive, however. She was stopped by the Garda who charged her with driving at seventy-five m.p.h. through a thirty m.p.h. limit and taken to the nearest police station. In the waiting area, handcuffed to two detectives, Sarah sat, looking like a prematurely aged crone. 'Eileen,' she called out as her cousin entered the area. 'What are you in for?'

'Speeding.'

Sarah had neglected herself for so long that her wits were no longer about her.

'Do you mean selling the drug, speed?'

'No, no, no, you fool, driving too fast,' Eileen replied, adding, 'What are you in for?'

'Murder,' said Sarah.

The women were jerked to their feet and taken to separate cells.

* * *

After a remand in custody, Sarah underwent a short trial and although it transpired that she was very eccentric, no diagnosis of mental illness could be labelled upon her. She was sentenced to thirty years imprisonment.

Her behaviour in prison caused trouble and concern to the authorities. In the canteen, she ate copiously for the sake of her baby. Then she would return to her cell, which she shared with two other prisoners.

She alienated her cell-mates. She told them nothing, either about herself or her relationship with her uncle. When they questioned her, she did not reply, causing them to dislike her even more. She still had the gold locket round her neck and decided that she would only be at ease in her own company.

Her strategy was intelligent. First, she poured a slop bucket over one of the warders. Then she bit another warder's finger when she had, if foolishly, tried to remove her locket. She was put in solitary that afternoon. There was a life-sized crucifix in the spartan cell. She turned her back on it and prayed to Sir Jasper Montrose: 'O, Jas, who art born, half Cossack and half bear, let there be someone to hear my screams when I go into labour.'

She went into labour two days later. Her screams were indeed heard by the warders. One of them, formerly a nurse, entered her cell and had her transferred to the prison hospital where she gave birth the following morning.

Sarah felt an initial surge of happiness, on seeing the screaming, purple creature that had been wrapped in a shawl and placed into her arms. She became instantly overjoyed on seeing that she had a living, baby daughter. She was thankful that the baby was alive and hoped that she could mould her into a miniature version of herself.

Suddenly, she felt ill. She experienced a feeling so alarming that she thought she was going to die. Her blood pressure had plummeted dramatically. She started to have palpitations. An instinct told her that her time was up.

'Please, please, listen,' she called out. 'Give me some paper and a pen! Hurry, I think I'm dying.'

One of the prison hospital nurses granted her request. She helped Sarah to sit up a bit so that she could write.

'Thank you. I'll stay with my baby now.'

Sarah felt increasingly ill. She was only just able to write:

> To my daughter whom I name Alandra Varinia:
>
> You will never know me because I am about to die. You were born of the glorious union of Seamus O'Rafferty and myself. Read this when you have learnt your letters and if you still can't read properly, ask someone to read it to you. Be brave and bold to the end, like your mother before you. Learn well the virtue of loyalty.
>
> I leave to you my locket, bearing the picture of my God, Sir Jasper Montrose. He was a famous man and there will be books about him in any library. Take this locket in your hand each night, open it and pray and he will hear you.
>
> Don't expect me to tell you the difference between right and wrong. I don't even know it myself. And don't expect me to tell you the difference between truth and lies because that is something I have never known either. I may not be a good woman but you have not lacked a mother's love.

The pen fell from her hand. Sarah held her daughter to her chest and died.

The death certificate recorded fatally low blood pressure.

Sarah was buried in an unnamed pauper's grave and in later life it was only Alandra Varinia and her half-siblings who either knew or cared that she had ever existed.

Part VI

The Biddle Family Again

A long time hence, at Mulligan Manor, Hannah Biddle, the more robust of the twin sisters, became aware that her father had fallen down the ladder leading to the loft, broken his neck and died. Mary, her sister, was still in the attic and refused to come down. Hannah was left with her exasperatingly neurotic mother.

'I don't know what's going on,' said Hannah to her mother. 'I don't think there's any point in leaving here but I do feel that we ought to get a medium in to do a séance and after that, an exorcist.'

Hannah had not told her mother that her father was dead for fear that she would do something foolish. Hannah dragged Biddle's body downstairs and hid it in the study.

Betsie Miles, a British-born Dubliner, was a professional medium. She was neatly, if unfashionably dressed, in a grey, tweed suit and matching hat. She was abnormally thin and waif-like. Hannah greeted her and her secretary as they walked up the drive. Betsy was carrying a little dispatch box in her hand. She and her secretary walked into the house at the back entrance, through to the hall, and removed their hats.

'The whole place is absolutely alive with it!' Betsy gasped.

'With what?' asked Hannah.

'I feel it's all coming from the linoleum-floored corridor at the back of the house, but we will examine this later at the séance. Have you, by any chance, a modest glass of sherry?'

'Yes, of course.' Hannah went into the study and brought a glass of sherry to Betsie who was in the living room.

After they had eaten, Hannah, her mother, Alice, Betsie and the secretary set up a table in the hall and turned down the lighting. Every member of the party laid their hands, palms downwards, on a circular, wooden table. Betsie did so first and then raised her hands an inch above the table. Her hands wandered in the air as she started speaking.

'Is there someone who lived in this house who is not at peace?'

There was no answer. The temperature of the room dropped and although the windows were closed, an unearthly gust of coldness swept through the four women and made them shudder.

'Can you tell me whose soul is not at rest?'

The word 'No' was passed to Betsie but she knew that the truth was not being told.

'Are you not at peace, Melissa O'Rafferty?'

A gust of wind crashed against Betsie so ferociously that she fell to the floor.

'I can smell drink in here. It is so overpowering that I can hardly breathe. Did you consume large quantities of alcohol in this house, Melissa O'Rafferty?'

The 'Yes' message was passed to Betsie who shouted the word. Her secretary wrote 'Yes' on a sheet of paper, covering the entire page and pushed it violently to the centre of the table.

'Isn't that an awful waste of paper?' bleated Alice.

'Don't make daft remarks like that and keep your mouth shut!' shouted Hannah.

'Melissa O'Rafferty, did your drinking have any ill affect on people living in this house?'

Again, Betsie heard the word 'Yes' and yet another gust of wind passed through the room. Her secretary wrote the single word once more on another piece of paper which she pushed to the centre of the table.

'If we have two "Yesses" in a row, can't you just write "Yes" on the bottom of the first piece of paper saying "Yes"?' said Alice.

Hannah restrained her temper. Betsie turned to Alice. 'The more you talk, the more you show your ignorance. This is the way in which a séance is conducted. Quite apart from that, it is my paper that is being "wasted", not yours.'

Betsie continued.

'Did you die in this house?' Again, came the affirmative answer which her secretary wrote down.

'How did you die, Melissa O'Rafferty?'

Suddenly, Betsie abandoned her voice and took on Melissa's. The others were terrified.

'I ground up some glass with a rolling pin in the kitchen. I washed it down with a bottle of gin. Suddenly, I had an agonizing pain in the stomach. I meant to go outside the house for help but I fell down and don't remember any more.'

'Did you fall in the narrow corridor at the back of the house with the linoleum floor?' asked Betsie.

There was a long pause. Betsie repeated the message invading her psyche.

'Yes!' Melissa gasped.

'All right,' said Hannah aggressively at the end of the séance, out of her mother's hearing. 'My father is dead. My twin sister is in the attic and won't come down. You've done nothing to right my family's problems. When are you sending for an exorcist?'

'An exorcist can do nothing, Miss Hannah. The damage is too severe. All I can do is insist on your leaving this house.'

'What about my sister?'

'Your sister is her own agent. Either you get her down by force or you leave her in the attic.'

'You're a crook and a charlatan. You insult me by thinking that you can frighten me with your magic powers. Send me your bill but don't expect me to pay it,' shouted Hannah.

Betsie and her secretary left the house in a rage. Hannah went to Dublin in search of love and adventure, taking with her the family's pet Labrador, Toby. Alice, her mother, was found by the cook one morning, lying on her back, staring vacantly into space. She was finally confined to a mental institution and has never been seen again.

The house stands where it stood but has not been inhabited since. The skeleton of Mary Biddle, who starved to death, still lies on the attic floor.

As for the fate of Alandra Varinia, that is another story.